Great Lakes Wolves

ACCEPTING THE ALPHA

JJ BLACK

Accepting the Alpha
ISBN # 978-1-78184-732-9
©Copyright JJ Black 2014
Cover Art by Posh Gosh ©Copyright January 2014
Interior text design by Claire Siemaszkiewicz
Totally Bound Publishing

Published in 2014 by Totally Bound Publishing, Newland House, The Point, Weaver Road, Lincoln, LN6 3QN, United Kingdom.

Totally Bound Publishing is an imprint of Total-E-Ntwined Limited.

ACCEPTING THE ALPHA

Dedication

For Jessica, who believed and for Jenny, who made it real. Thank you.

Chapter One

"I can't believe I let you talk me into this," Eli huffed, irritation clear in his voice.

"Oh, come on! You told me you wanted to meet the local Alpha and I wanted to go to a club. Kellan owns the club, so I see this as a win-win situation. It's like multi-tasking."

Eli stared at his friend in disbelief. "You brought me to a gay bar, asshole. In case you failed to notice, I'm straight. You honestly think this is the best place for me to approach the Alpha about joining his pack?"

"Are you kidding?" Jai scoffed. "I can't think of a better place than the club. The atmosphere here is way more relaxed than a formal meeting would be. Besides, you know as well as I do that it's always better to approach an Alpha when he's in a good mood." Jai leered, waggling his eyebrows. "Trust me. Kellan is always in a good mood here."

Eli glared at his best friend. "Don't you think the fact that I'm not gay is going to count against me in a place like this?"

Shaking his head, Jai gave him a look of disgust. "Not everyone in the club is gay, douche. Sephora is the official gathering place for the pack. Everyone comes here to hang out—gay, straight or bi. Besides," he added smugly, "I already told Kellan you would be here tonight. He's looking forward to meeting you." With a smirk on his face, Jai turned away, effectively dismissing Eli and his nervous rant, to check out the night's offerings. By the look on his face, he definitely liked what he saw.

Letting out a weary sigh, Eli leaned back in his seat, taking another look around the club. At a glance, it didn't look that much different than any other club he had been in back home. The main floor of the building looked more like a sports bar than a gay club. A long, oak bar took up one wall with large flat-screen TVs mounted down the wall above. Tall, round tables filled the central floor, while pool tables and dartboards had residence at the back of the room. Without the higher than average number of same-sex couples holding hands or snuggling in booths, it would have been difficult to single it out as a gay club.

The real action, however, could be found upstairs in the dance club portion of the bar, aptly nicknamed Temptation. In Temptation, clothing seemed to be optional, as showcased by the writhing masses of men and women pressed together in a seemingly endless display of sweat-slick skin and groping hands. Although complete nudity was not allowed, it seemed the patrons of the club liked to push the rule to the limit. Most of the inhabitants of the dance floor were showing more skin than they had covered, be the men or women. For as far as the eye could see, there was glistening skin pressed tight to glistening skin. Large male hands groping hard male flesh. Female lips laving and teasing the feminine curve of a neck. The occasional male-female couple could be found to round out the group, but they were most definitely in the minority.

As the music blared and the bass rumbled like thunder, the bodies on the floor gyrated together like limbs of a massive beast. Twisting, turning, wrapped together in intimate embrace. The air was thick with lust and made Eli aware of just how long it had been since he'd slaked his own. The aphrodisiac quality of it was not lost on him.

Taking in the sights, Eli was surprised when he found himself checking out just as many of the male pleasure seekers as female. He tried to dismiss it, convinced it was nothing more than casual appreciation. Just one man recognizing the good looks of another. So what if he focused a little too long on the rippled planes of a male abdomen or had the strangest desire to snag a small masculine nipple between his teeth before laving the sting away with his tongue? He wanted to chalk it up to a mere side effect of being immersed in this new environment, where sexuality was not just encouraged, but accentuated and put on display. He'd never experienced the kind of sexual freedom he observed within the walls of Temptation. Surrounded by such overt expressions of homosexuality, he tried to remind himself that this type of display couldn't possibly turn him on. However, as his pants started to become uncomfortably tight, he had a feeling that he wasn't being completely honest with himself. Unnerved by his unwanted arousal, Eli shivered, turning back to the bar and his beer. Taking a long pull from the bottle, he spared a glance over at Jai. His friend, ever on the prowl, was too busy taking in the buffet of naked flesh to notice.

Eli took advantage of Jai's moment of distraction to observe him objectively. Jai had always garnered a lot of attention, both male and female, when they went out. Despite having been friends since infancy, he realized he had never taken the time to see what all the fuss was about.

As teenagers, they had been nicknamed Day and Night, for their opposing looks. They were nearly identical in height and build, reaching around six foot three and just over two hundred pounds. That, however, was where the similarities ended. Jai embodied everything that was light, with his golden hair, sun-kissed skin and eyes the color of a cloudless summer day. With his hard, muscled body encased in dark denim and a collared shirt the color of his eyes, he resembled a golden god. Eli had to admit, he could definitely understand all the attention his friend was garnering at the club. The man practically glowed, drawing people in like moths to a flame.

Eli, on the other hand, personified all that was night. His hair was black, so dark that when the sun hit it just right there appeared to be blue highlights streaked throughout. He wore it short in the back and sides, leaving the front just long enough to tease the arch of his brows. His eyes were also blue but the blue-black of twilight. Dressed as he was in a pair of threadbare jeans, a tight, gray T-shirt and scuffed motorcycle boots, Jai and Eli really did look like opposite sides of the same coin.

A change in his friend's demeanor brought back his focus. Looking closely, Eli watched as his best friend's eyes lit up like Christmas morning. A grin spread across his face and he practically vibrated with happiness. Curious to see the cause of Jai's excitement, Eli followed the direction of his gaze toward the front entrance of the club.

Walking through the doorway was a group of some of the largest men Eli had ever seen in his life. Eli was far from small, but in comparison to these men, he seemed almost dainty. They were not just tall, but had thick, muscular bodies as well. With their wide shoulders and powerful frames, they were built like defensive linemen. As they walked, muscles bulged beneath tight T-shirts that looked as though they were moments away from complete disintegration from the strain. Their whole demeanor screamed — *Back the fuck away!*

Noticing Eli's perusal, the largest member of the group chose that moment to glance his way. Eli was shocked by the sheer size of the man. He had to be at least six and a half feet tall and close to three hundred pounds. His well-formed body was covered in finely honed sinew. The man was built like a brick shithouse. His hair was a rich, chocolate brown and long enough that it was pulled back into a ponytail at the base of his neck. His black dress shirt was untucked, with the sleeves pulled back to mid forearm, showcasing powerful arms and prominent veins that, for a moment, Eli had a nearly overwhelming urge to trace with his tongue. Power rolled off the big man in waves and crackled along Eli's skin, making his wolf perk up and take notice.

At a glance, he looked relaxed and ready for a night of drinking and dancing with friends, but on closer inspection, Eli could sense his alertness. The predator within was anything but idle. The dark Aviators he wore were probably meant to camouflage the way his eyes scanned the room for any possible threat, but Eli recognized the subtle shifts of his body and occasional tilt of his head as signs of his vigilance. The large man was ready to take action at a moment's notice. This was without a doubt the Alpha, Kellan Reeves. Although he couldn't see it, Eli could feel the heavy weight of the Alpha's stare. The man's gaze seemed to burn right into him. His body heated and a shiver worked its way through his frame.

A smirk formed on the man's lips, telling Eli that Alpha Reeves had noticed his inspection, as well as his reaction to him. Eli's cheeks flamed scarlet as embarrassment made his heart speed to a gallop in his chest. He tried to break eye contact with the larger man but felt frozen in place. The smile on the Alpha's face only grew larger as Eli's embarrassment grew. Eli watched as Alpha Reeves slowly ran his tongue over his lips, leaving behind an enticing sheen of moisture. He felt a familiar tightening in his balls, and his cock hardened to the point of pain. He bit back a moan as confusion warred with his unwanted arousal.

What the hell?

While Eli knew many shifters who were attracted to both sexes and had no issue switching between the two, he had never been even remotely attracted to another male, let alone got hard from just an appraising look from one. Something about this man, however, appealed to Eli on a level he had never experienced before. From his high cheekbones, strong muscled body and rugged good looks, Kellan Reeves had him nearly panting like a dog in heat.

Eli didn't want to examine his attraction too closely. He had enough on his plate without adding in an unexpected attraction to the local Alpha. Joining the pack had to be his number one priority. He had already gone too long as a lone wolf. Much longer and he could become a danger to himself or to others. Wolf shifters were not meant to be solitary creatures. The longer they were without a pack, the closer they came to going feral and attacking innocents. That wasn't something he was willing to risk, no matter how startled he was about the strange attraction he was feeling toward the Alpha.

The gorgeous man continued to hold his gaze until a club employee approached, causing him to break eye contact and release Eli from his thrall. A few words were shared between the two before the employee nodded and headed off in the direction of the bar. Sparing a glance back in their direction, the Alpha motioned for Jai and Eli to follow, then turned and made his way up the stairs, into the heart of Temptation. Eli could follow his progress from his seat at the bar easily. The crowd parted before him, like Moses and the Red Sea. A sigh escaped Eli's lips before he could cut it off. Turning back to the bar, he found Jai staring at him expectantly.

"Come on, man. Kellan's waiting on us. Let's go." He nudged Eli's arm with his elbow. "The guys with him are some of his Betas. He looks like he's in a good mood so this will be the perfect time to talk to him about joining the Pack."

Eli sighed. He knew what he had to do. It was just a matter of manning up and finding the courage to do it. He needed a pack and he needed to be near his best friend. Ever since their birth pack had forced Jai to leave after he'd announced he was gay, Eli had felt like a huge part of himself had been missing. Now, with his own exit from their old pack and the new separation from his brothers, Eli was more than grateful to have Jai back in his life. The Grand Rapids Pack was his best option at starting over.

Rising from his seat, he dutifully followed Jai through the teeming masses. As they worked their way through the crowd and up the stairs to Temptation, he could only hope that this would be the fresh start he needed.

As they reached the landing, Eli took a deep breath and almost took off running back down the stairs. If he had thought the pheromones were strong downstairs, this close they were nearly unbearable. He shook his head, trying to clear it, and promised himself that he would get laid before stepping into the club again. The scent of lust and sex in the building was too much for even a straight man to take. Unbidden, a vision of the Alpha's handsome face filled his mind, mocking him as arousal coursed through his body once again. *Okay*, he thought, chagrined, *maybe not completely straight.*

Despite his reservations, Eli realized that he wasn't completely against the idea of being with a man. Especially if that man was Kellan Reeves. Perhaps his lack of fear stemmed from his inherent easy-going personality. He'd never been one to stress about every little thing, preferring to just go with the flow. While being with a man was not an option he had ever considered before, it was something he was definitely thinking about now.

When they finally cleared the crowded dance floor, Eli saw that the entire back wall was lined with large, private booths. As they approached, he noticed, much to his shock, that most of them were filled with groups of people engaged in varying stages of intimacy. All of the booths were equipped with long, thick curtains that could be pulled out to completely enclose the booth, but most of the booths' inhabitants had forgone their use. The farther back they ventured, the more pornographic the acts became.

At one of the last tables, a thin, blond twink knelt on the floor as he swallowed the shaft of a much larger, dark-haired man. The brunet had a strong grip on his hair and was thrusting roughly into his mouth. As the smaller man devoured his thick, dripping cock, growls rolled out of his partner's mouth, as well as a graphic list of all the things he was going to do to the blond as soon as he was done fucking his mouth. The slim man moaned loudly, his eyes glazing over as the filthy words reached his ears. His cheeks hollowed as he started to suck more voraciously. The larger man's chest began to heave and just when Eli was sure he was going to blow, he ripped the blond off his cock, threw him down face first on the table, yanked down his pants and impaled him in one violent thrust. Eli winced at the brutality of it, but the smaller man seemed to love it, if the volume of his cries were any indication. Eli quickened his steps, desperate to insure he did not lose Jai in the crowd. Not accustomed to this kind of club, he was a little afraid of what else he might accidentally walk in on if he got lost in this place.

He was starting to wonder how big the club actually was when Jai came to a stop in front of a large lounge area in the back corner of the building. The entire area sat on an elevated platform that allowed for a clear line of sight of the rest of the club. Another massive booth was set against the back wall, and was flanked by a scattering of low sitting couches and chairs, all filled to capacity with a variety of pack members and partygoers.

As they approached, Eli recognized many of the men from their earlier entrance, although there were a number of new faces as well. Mixed in among the large Betas were a few small, waif-thin young men. All of them had smooth complexions and baby soft skin. Eli even noticed makeup on one or two. He mentally shook his head. He had never understood the appeal twinks had for some gay men. He had always figured if a man was gay, he would want to have sex with a man who was…well…manly. Eli could not grasp the appeal of the effeminate faces and reed-thin bodies. It seemed too much like having sex with a woman with a few extra parts. Then again, Eli had never considered the possibility that he would ever find another man sexually attractive until about five minutes earlier, so what did he really know about the mind of a gay man?

The small men giggled, girlishly fawning all over the larger men, and the guys seemed to be eating it up. Reaching out with his wolf senses told him that five of the large men were pack Betas, two of the twinks were low level pack members and the rest were all human. Add to that the numerous other men and women congregating around the area, and they had the makings of what could be a rowdy evening. The only thing that seemed to be missing from the equation was the Alpha. Frowning, Eli wondered where the big man had gone, until an extremely annoying peal of laughter drew his attention to the booth at the back of the room.

At first, all Eli could see was the slim back and short red hair of yet another twink. God, were they breeding them here or something? He had never seen so many in one place before. As he started to turn away, the small-bodied man was forcibly relocated and before him, in all his glory and pulsing power, sat a slightly annoyed-looking Alpha Kellan Reeves.

Moving to step up onto the dais, Jai and Eli were halted when a massive wall of muscle stepped in their way, blocking their path. Looking up, Eli was barely able to take in the image of a tall, dark-haired man with bulging muscles before Jai stepped in between them, red-faced and filled with righteous anger.

"What the fuck, Malachi?" Jai spat at the mountain of man standing before them. "Get the hell out of our way!"

"You, of course, may pass," the big man rumbled, his voice deep and rough like gravel, "but your friend will have to stay here." His tone brooked no arguments as he eyed Eli warily. Eli had no idea what the man thought he could possibly do to him. Eli had doubts a tank would have had any luck taking the gigantic man down.

Jai stomped his foot before giving Malachi a solid punch to the arm. Eli cringed, half expecting to hear his friend's bones crunching on impact. "We have an appointment with Kellan, you big asshole! If you don't believe me, why don't you go ask our fearless leader? While you're there, you can explain why you're being so unwelcoming to a prospective new pack member. I'm sure he's gonna love that," Jai added, with a glare.

Malachi, sighed, a look of defeat plastered on his face. "Calm down and wait here. I've got to go check it out with the boss," he grumbled, trudging off in the direction of the big booth. A few hushed words were spoken before Malachi made his way back to where Jai and Eli were waiting. Jai had an expectant look on his face and was tapping his foot, obnoxiously, for effect. When Malachi stopped in front of him, Jai just stared silently into his face…waiting.

After a moment of silence, Malachi let out an enormous sigh. "Jesus, Jai! Why do you have to be such a prick all the time? You know I'm just doing my job. How bad would you feel if I just let anybody in and then somebody took a shot at the boss, huh?"

"Malachi, Kellan stands a better chance of me taking a shot at him than Eli. As a matter of fact, I think about taking him out at least once or twice a week. If he wants to be a pansy about it, he should really be more worried about me. I'm not as harmless as I look." Jai shot Malachi a look that, Eli assumed, was supposed to come across as dangerous but really did a better job of making his friend look slightly deranged.

The men were silent for a moment before breaking down laughing like a couple of loons. By the time they had regained some small amount of control over themselves, both Jai and Malachi had red faces, slightly puffy and wet with tears.

A fond smile broke out on Malachi's face and he reached out to pat Jai affectionately on the back. "You're a good guy, Jai. Funny as hell and always full of piss and vinegar. Always makes for an interesting combination." Throwing a smile in Eli's direction, Malachi motioned them forward. "I got the okay from the boss, so you guys are good to go in. Enjoy your night."

When Malachi stepped back out of their way, they made their way up onto the dais, before Eli looked around and found himself instantly locking eyes with the Alpha. The sight of the man before him left Eli momentarily breathless. Standing this close to the Alpha was like a punch to the gut. From a distance, he had been handsome. Up close, where Eli could appreciate the finer details that made up his appearance, the man was absolutely stunning. His hair was not just brown, as he had originally assumed, but a mix of blonds, browns and gold. He'd removed his sunglasses so Eli was now able to see that his eyes were a vibrant shade of green, like the color of new spring leaves. He was also much bigger up close. Whether it was his presence, his build or a combination of the two, he seemed to fill the room. He had to have Eli's own six foot three beat by at least four inches. This was the first time in his life Eli had ever felt small and Eli was uncomfortable with how vulnerable he felt in the presence of the big man. The realization that, if it came down to it, Kellan Reeves could take him out without much effort did little to settle Eli's ragged nerves. The Alpha's scent wasn't helping much, either.

The man's scent was a mix between a soft spring breeze and something spicy and warm. It was fresh, clean and definitely not unpleasant, if the state of Eli's erection was any means to judge. His wolf, however, was having major issues with it. Eli could feel its hackles rise as his beast fought to be released. With his close proximity to the Alpha, Eli barely managed to bite back the growl trying to work its way out of his throat. He bit the inside of his cheek hard enough to draw blood, hoping to distract his wolf from the man sitting before them. While he could normally understand his wolf's thoughts and feelings, at that moment, they were chaotic and unclear. The fact that he couldn't tell if his inner wolf wanted to fight the Alpha or fuck him left Eli feeling unsettled and scared.

The smirk that appeared on Kellan's face let Eli know he was not hiding his internal struggle as well as he'd thought. Alpha Reeves stared at him for a moment and Eli again felt frozen by the power of his gaze. The Alpha's expression softened briefly before he broke eye contact, turning to address Jai. The smile that lit his face clearly showed the affection the man had for Eli's friend. It made his respect for the Alpha grow.

"Jai, I'm glad you made it tonight. You've been missed this week." His voice was dark and smooth like whiskey. "By some of us more than others..." His gaze flicked to the side, settling briefly on a dark-haired man sitting to his right. He wasn't quite as large as Kellan, but he still had to be over six and a half feet. While his size should have made him menacing, Eli sensed a gentleness in him that was completely at odds with the powerful man before him. The man looked up briefly, eyes flicking toward Jai before quickly dropping back to his lap, where he was fiddling with his cell phone.

"Jai," the man acknowledged quietly, without looking up.

"Dylan." Jai smirked. The expression on his friend's face was one Eli had never seen before. Equal parts longing and challenge. He knew instantly that there was something between the two men, but neither seemed willing to acknowledge it.

The silence that followed their greeting was awkward for everyone. Kellan, apparently impatient with their silence, snorted rudely before turning his attention back to Jai and Eli. "So, Jai, is this him?"

"Yeah, man. This is him. Kel, I'd like to introduce you to my almost brother, Elijah Steele. Eli, this is Kellan Reeves, Alpha of the Grand Rapids Pack."

When Kellan stared silently at him, Eli took that as his sign to make his move. Tilting his head briefly to the side in a show of respect, he stepped closer, arm outstretched. "Pleased to meet you, Alpha Reeves." When his voice came out deep and strong, he couldn't have been more grateful. The last thing he needed was for the Alpha to think he was timid or weak. He needed to be accepted into this pack, and first impressions lasted a lifetime.

Kellan watched him curiously for what seemed like an eternity before he rose and clasped his hand in return. The moment their hands touched, Eli felt like he had been stuck with a cattle prod. An electric, burning sensation worked its way up his arm then through the rest of his body, leaving an odd tingling awareness in its wake. After a brief hesitation, Kellan released his grip. The Alpha's face gave nothing away, so instead of shaking out his arm like he really wanted to do, Eli merely flexed his fingers and lowered them down to his side.

"The pleasure is all mine, Eli," Kellan replied, his smirk back in place, retaking his seat. "So, what brings you to Grand Rapids?"

Looking around at the group surrounding them, Eli's unease grew. He'd never been quick to open up around strangers. It would be hard enough having to come clean with Kellan. There was no way he'd be able to dump his private pain out for all of these people to see.

"I was actually hoping to set up a private meeting with you to discuss my…situation. I would hate to interrupt your evening out." Eli's eyes flicked briefly to the redhead that was now strategically pouting next to Kellan. "If it works for you, maybe we could set something up for later in the week…?" He kept his eyes trained respectfully on the ground as he fought to catch his breath. God, why the hell did this guy fuck with his head so bad? He honestly had no explanation for it. Eli had never had this kind of reaction to another wolf. It was driving him crazy.

A look of understanding appeared on Kellan's face. The answering smile the Alpha gave him was lazy and relaxed. "No worries, Eli. You're not interrupting anything special."

Oh, burn on the Ginger.

"I always have time for pack business. Why don't you go snag a drink from the bar, on the house, of course, and we'll get right down to the nitty-gritty of it, all right?" While a cocky grin twisted his lips, there was warmth in his eyes that assured Eli that he really did want to help him if he could. With a nod, Eli rose from his seat and headed toward the bar, a small smile curling his lips and the hope of having a home again slowly growing in his chest.

Chapter Two

Kellan waited until Eli was out of earshot before turning on Jai. "Is he claimed?" he growled, urgency creeping into his tone.

Jai studied Kellan in shock. "No, Kel, he doesn't have a mate, but he's also not gay."

Relief filled Kellan at the news that the gorgeous man had no other entanglements. While nothing would have stopped him from claiming what was his, an existing relationship would have made things more difficult. Thankfully, fate had practically delivered his mate on a silver platter.

Mate? He couldn't believe his luck. Jai was always talking about the elusive Eli. He was constantly regaling them with stories of their childhood and all the trouble they had caused as pups. While Kellan had found the stories amusing, he had never given much thought to the friend Jai held in such high regard. He couldn't believe how much time he had wasted with his mate simply by not taking a more active interest in meeting the man who meant so much to one of his closest friends. It was painfully obvious that he had been spending too much time lately wrapped up in his own trivial bullshit. The anger and regret building inside him, caused by his own short-sightedness, made him want to kick his own ass.

All of that was about to change. Eli was within his reach and there was no doubt in his mind that he belonged to Kellan. While the man being straight was an unfortunate hiccup in his plans, he could work around it. Eli wouldn't be the first man Kellan had been with who had claimed to only be attracted to women, but he would be the last. They all started out with the same spiel about 'men just not doing it for them', but it wasn't long after that they had all ended up moaning and writhing on the end of his dick. From what Jai had told him of their birth pack, where same sex unions were not only frowned upon but banned entirely, Eli had likely never been exposed to same sex mating. Kellan knew it was only a matter of time before he had Eli right where he wanted him.

Despite his upbringing, Kellan could already sense the curiosity building in the other man. He had seen his mate checking out the club's other patrons, as well as Kellan himself. The thought of being the only man to ever have the pleasure of touching Eli had Kellan's cock filling with painful speed. He winced as he tried to adjust the growing bulge in his pants. He was hopeful that, with a little luck, he would be able to convince his mate to see things his way before the week was over.

A moment's doubt filled him, however, as he looked on at the wolf fate had chosen to be his partner in life. He had to admit, he was a little surprised by the sheer size and presence of the other man. Kellan tended to pick bed partners that were both physically and emotionally submissive to him. As an Alpha, it was something his wolf demanded. Eli was a strong, dominant wolf in his own right. Kellan was worried Eli's beast would not allow him to submit to Kellan, the way the Alpha needed him to. He mulled over the issue briefly, before dismissing his concerns. He was the Alpha and Eli was his destined mate. The gods would not give him a mate unable to meet his needs. Eli would learn to submit and Kellan would enjoy teaching him how.

Kellan followed Eli's progress as his mate gracefully worked his way through the crowd, enjoying the play of muscles, as they bunched and flexed with every move of Eli's hard-packed body. His mate was magnificent and it quickly became clear to Kellan that he was not the only one who noticed. To his intense displeasure, his man was stopped numerous times by both men and women trying every trick in the book to draw him onto the dance floor. The blush blooming on his mate's cheeks was enticing, as he good-naturedly tried to fight off their advances.

Kellan couldn't fault the others their appreciation of the man. With his tall, muscled frame and dark good looks, he was nothing like the men Kellan usually took to his bed. The definition of his hard body was easy to see through the thin material of his T-shirt, and the worn jeans he was barely wearing were molded to his ass like a second skin. They were so thin, Kellan could swear he saw a hint of ass peeking through them. The possibility of his mate going commando had him nearly salivating.

Kellan continued to watch as a still blushing Eli was dragged onto the dance floor and into the embrace of a large cat shifter from one of the local prides. A snarl escaped Kellan and his hackles rose, causing Jai to throw him another appraising look, but Kellan was past the point of caring. Looking was one thing, but no one got to touch what was his!

After pushing away from the table, he stormed down the stairs and stalked his mate across the room. As he neared, he could clearly make out the large hands of the cat trying to get a firm grip on his mate's ass. Sensing his mate's discomfort, Kellan released the growl that had been building in his chest.

Both men's heads jerked up at the sound. The look on Kellan's face must have been enough to relay his unhappiness because the cat was across the room almost faster than even Kellan's wolf sight could register. The relief he felt from Eli warmed him, helping to calm his still agitated wolf. That he had successfully protected his mate only increased Kellan's need to claim him. Without a conscious thought, Kellan grabbed Eli's hand and gently pulled him into his body.

While Eli was hesitant, his eyes were filled with only confusion. There was no fear or disgust, which helped to further soothe Kellan's wolf. As he looked down into his mate's midnight eyes, he felt himself drowning in their depths. Wrapping his arms around the smaller man's waist, he drew Eli closer until they were chest to chest, pressed together so tightly that Kellan could feel every dip and bump of his mate's rippled abdomen. It also meant he was very aware of the massive hard-on Eli's jeans were in no way helping to conceal. From what he could feel, the man had to be rockin' at least eight inches and Kellan couldn't wait to get a taste.

"Oh, darlin'," he drawled, running a hot hand down the front of Eli's jeans, giving the impressive bulge a firm squeeze, "is that for me?"

Eli blushed impossibly redder and tried to take a step back, but Kellan kept his arms wrapped tightly around him, giving him no chance of escape. "Alpha... This place... The pheromones..." he stammered adorably. Kellan watched as Eli forced himself to stop and take a breath. He lowered his eyes in a show of respect and deference. "I apologize, sir. It's...been a while. I didn't think that all this"—he waved an arm at the room—"would affect me so strongly. I'll try not to let it happen again."

Kellan placed a finger under Eli's chin and forced him to look him in the eye. "Don't fight it on my account. In fact, I seem to have found myself in a similar situation." Grabbing Eli's hand, he shoved it down until their joined hands were cupping Kellan's heavy erection. The moment Eli's hand came in contact with his cock, Kellan felt a shockwave jolt through his body, setting every nerve ending on high alert. He rolled his hips and began to gently thrust into Eli's hot palm. At first, Eli had no reaction. He looked like he could have been carved out of stone, he was so still. Kellan was about to give up hope of any participation on Eli's behalf until he felt a tentative squeeze around his engorged shaft.

For a moment, he thought he had imagined the touch, but then he felt it again, less hesitant than before. Opening the eyes he hadn't realized he had shut, he was met with eyes so passion-blown, they had gone completely black. The look on Eli's face was a mix of curiosity and hunger that nearly stole Kellan's breath. He needed to get closer. Taking a chance, he leaned in, licking the seam of Eli's soft lips. Although he got no response, the taste of his mate drove him on. "Open up for me, baby. Let me in."

Pushing forward for another taste, Kellan was pleased to find that Eli could follow instruction. The man's lips were relaxed and parted just slightly, but it was enough that Kellan was able to slip his tongue between them and into the depths of his mate's sweet mouth. Kellan lapped up his flavor as he thrust his tongue deeper, essentially fucking Eli's mouth with his invading muscle. He didn't think there was any way he could have been more turned on until he felt the tentative touch of Eli's tongue on his own. It took all his years of carefully honed control to keep from blowing his load in his pants, right in the middle of the club.

Their kiss continued in a fevered mating of lips, teeth and tongues. A moan worked its way up from Eli's chest, but Kellan swallowed it down, not wanting anyone else to have the pleasure of hearing his mate's passion-filled cries. Unfortunately, the need for air eventually became too strong to ignore, forcing Kellan to pull back. The blissed out expression on Eli's face had Kellan fighting the urge to drag him off to the nearest dark corner and mount him. Only the knowledge that Eli wasn't ready for anything that intense kept Kellan from doing something that might forever ruin his relationship with his mate.

Kellan placed one last, chaste kiss on his lips, then turned and steered a still dazed Eli toward the bar to get their long forgotten drinks. By the time they made it to the bar and placed their drink order, Eli was back in control of himself and had visibly pulled away from Kellan. While he had known that it was the most likely reaction to what they had done, Kellan had hoped that his mate would easily adjust to the fact that he was destined to be mated to another man. Sighing, he grabbed drinks from the bar before heading back in the direction of their table, trusting Eli to follow.

Everyone was still lounging around when they returned. Dropping their haul on the table, Eli and Kellan watched in amusement as the others fought over the remaining drinks. When the icy beverages had all been claimed and everyone had settled back into their own conversations, Kellan turned his attention back to Eli who was studiously staring at the scarred wood table top. Shaking his head, Kellan decided to allow Eli his temporary escape. Instead, he would use this time to start making strides toward learning more about his mate and what had driven him to come to Grand Rapids.

"Everything seems under control out here. Eli, why don't we head back to my office for that talk?" While Kellan posed the statement as a question to ease his mate's nervousness, they both knew better. Alphas didn't ask questions, they gave orders.

Eli looked to Jai who gave him an indifferent shrug, before turning away to take another sip of his drink, effectively forcing Eli to make his own choice. Eli paused for a moment before giving a look of resignation and preparing to follow Kellan from the room. Kellan's expression softened slightly, approval pouring off him. Eli's response to Kellan's request just proved to Kellan that the man already trusted him. It was a good sign that this mating just might work out without too much trouble, after all. As soon as Eli learned to trust himself and his feelings for Kellan, their mating would be on solid ground.

When others made a move to follow, Kellan waved them off. "Stay. We'll only be a few minutes. We have some things to talk about, privately." His Betas took the order in stride, immediately turning back to their previous activities. Unfortunately, Tracy, his now ex-lover, didn't seem to appreciate the order, if his crossed arms and the scowl marring his delicate face were any indication. Unfortunately for Tracy, Kellan didn't have the time or inclination to deal with his drama. All he wanted was to be alone with his mate away from the noise and the crowd of the club.

Kellan led Eli from the lounge without a backward glance. He could sense his mate's unease but hoped, if he kept things professional, his mate would relax and talk freely in his presence. They headed down a short hallway before ending up at the large black door of his office. He could practically feel the relief pouring off Eli at the realization that they were still within yelling distance of his friend. Kellan tried not to let that knowledge upset him, but it hurt to know that his mate didn't trust him enough to be completely alone with him. Kellan assured himself that, before long, he would earn Eli's trust and that, in turn, Eli would accept their mating without reservations.

Pushing open the door, Kellan led them into his office. Glancing wistfully at the couch, he moved to take a seat behind his desk, hoping that it would put his new mate at ease. Without prompting, Eli took a seat in one of the chairs flanking the desk, seeming to relax just a bit further. Kellan didn't like the distance between them, but judging by Eli's reaction, he knew he had made the right choice.

"Eli," he began, attempting to ease them into conversation, "why don't you tell me a little about yourself?"

"What would you like to know?" Eli's expression was guarded.

"Let's start with something I've been dying to know, since the minute I met you. How did you and Jai meet, and, more importantly, how did you become friends? I don't believe I've ever met two people who were more different. He's often told us stories of your exploits, but I guess I always assumed you were more..." Kellan hesitated, looking for a word that wouldn't insult his mate.

"Flamboyant?" Eli offered, a small smile quirking his beautiful lips.

"Yes," Kellan confirmed, flashing his mate a smile in return. "That is a perfect description."

Eli shook his head. "We were born two weeks apart and our parents have been best friends for as long as I can remember. We literally grew up together. I love him, like I love my brothers. He's family."

"You are very lucky, then," Kellan replied, softly. "I always wished for siblings, but it wasn't meant to be."

Eli laughed. "I don't know about lucky. Cursed is probably a better description. The five of us drove each other, and everyone else in a fifteen mile radius, crazy. Jai was always the ring leader because he always had the best ideas. He has the most scheming mind of anyone I've ever met."

It was Kellan's turn to laugh. "That much has not changed. He is still a master schemer."

"Has he been behaving himself?" Eli asked, hopefully.

"For the most part." Kellan smirked. "Although, he's got one of my Betas completely tied up in knots."

"Dylan?" Eli guessed.

"You've got it in one."

"What's going on with them?" Eli asked, curiously.

Kellan paused, trying to put his finger on the best way to describe the problem. He sighed. "To be perfectly blunt about it, I believe that they are mates."

"But that's a good thing... Isn't it?"

"Yes. Normally, it would be an amazing thing. They are two of my closest friends and some of the best men I have ever had the pleasure to know."

Eli looked at him, in confusion. "Then, I don't understand the problem."

Kellan rubbed his hands over his face, sighing tiredly. "For whatever reason, neither of them will come out and claim the other. There was a rumor circulating a few months ago that Jai was going to announce that they were mates, but it never happened. I've tried talking to both of them about it, but neither is willing to discuss it."

"Poor Jai," Eli murmured sadly. "There would have to be a damn good reason for Jai not to claim his mate, if he knew about him. Even when we were pups, he'd always talk about wanting to meet his mate. He deserves to be happy. I hope they are able to work it out."

"As do I," Kellan agreed. "So tell me, if you and Jai are so close, why did you stay in Mason after Jai came to Grand Rapids and joined my pack? By the way the two of you act, I doubt there are very many things you've done apart."

Eli smiled, but it didn't reach his eyes. "Staying behind after the Pack forced Jai to leave was one of the hardest things I've ever done. I would have liked nothing better than to pack my shit and leave with him, but it wasn't my time. I knew Jai was coming to you, so I knew he was going to be okay. My Pack, on the other hand, still needed me. I couldn't leave them."

"What about the Betas and Gammas of your old Pack? Surely your father, the Alpha, had them to help him with the Pack. Why did he need you so desperately?" Something wasn't adding up with the situation Eli was describing. Kellan needed to understand what had happened.

"I never said my father needed me, Alpha Reeves. I said my Pack needed me." Eli's words were quiet, barely a whisper.

If Kellan hadn't had enhanced hearing, he would have missed the words entirely. Leaning across his desk, he cupped Eli's cheek with his large hand, gently rubbing his thumb across his cheekbone. Eli leaned into the touch, just enough for Kellan to register the movement. "Your Alpha, your Pack. Isn't that the same thing, E?"

Eli rubbed his face gently against Kellan's palm, startlingly reminiscent of a kitten, instead of the wolf he actually was. After one last pass against Kellan's palm, Eli tilted his head to meet Kellan's green-eyed scrutiny. "Not in the Mason Pack."

Kellan wasn't sure what Eli was trying to say, but he had a pretty good idea that, whatever it was, it wasn't good. "What does that mean, E?"

Kellan was hoping to get to the bottom of it, when the door was thrown open and Tracy marched into the room like he owned the place. Eli jerked back until Kellan's hand was no longer touching his face. Before his eyes, he could see Eli shutting down and his walls going back up. Kellan wanted to curse Tracy for his rudeness and his stupidity. If they hadn't been friends for so long, he would have seriously considered having him punished for his behavior. Retaking his seat, he glared at the smaller man.

"What are you doing here, Tracy?" Kellan growled, his brow drawn down in anger.

"You were gone for so long," Tracy whined pitifully, "and I missed you." He flashed, what Kellan assumed was supposed to be a flirtatious smile before prancing across the room to him.

"As you can tell, I'm in a meeting. Eli has requested to join the Pack, and we have things to discuss."

Tracy glanced over at Eli, an expression of disdain clearly stamped across his face. Kellan couldn't understand this attitude from his ex. Maybe it had something to do with the very public make-out session Kellan and Eli had shared on the dance floor. Honestly, Kellan hadn't given Tracy much thought, at the time. He'd been too overwhelmed with the realization that Eli was his fated mate. Besides, his arrangement with Tracy had always been one of convenience, not love. Still, Kellan should have known it was too much to ask for Tracy to be cool with everything and not make a scene.

Kellan was completely lost in his own thoughts when Tracy, apparently irritated about being ignored, launched himself into Kellan's lap and proceeded to wrap his arms around his neck like he was a tree the smaller man wanted to climb.

While Kellan was far from pleased by Tracy's actions, he was surprised when he heard the low, eerie growl that slipped out from between Eli's clenched teeth and reverberated throughout the room. There was no missing the possessiveness in its tone. Kellan wasn't even sure Eli was aware he was doing it, but Tracy was.

The slender redhead glared over at Eli, his pale eyes gleaming with a malicious light. Kellan didn't know what the smaller man was thinking, but he was dangerously close to challenging a much stronger wolf.

"Kellan," Tracy sneered, "you need to teach the new puppy some manners. It seems he needs someone to show him his place."

"My place?" Eli snarled.

"Are you deaf? You talk to Kellan like you are his equal. Throw yourself at him." Tracy shook his head, his mouth turned down into a scowl. "He is the Alpha of the Grand Rapids Pack and you are nothing more than a vagrant, seeking to take advantage of his giving nature. You're not fit to stand before him. You should be on your knees."

"No," Kellan roared, "his place is at my side."

Tracy jerked back, like he'd been slapped. "You've got to be kidding! You're really gonna pick that homeless piece of trash over me?" The scorn in his voice was new, as was the rage smoldering in his eyes.

Before Kellan had a chance to defend his mate, Eli stepped forward, lips pulled back, canines bared, a warning growl resonating around them. Eli may not have been as big as Kellan—not many were—but he was still a very large male. He had a swimmer's build with wide shoulders, a narrow waist and layers on layers of muscle that Kellan couldn't wait to lick and taste. Eli had to have at least seventy-five pounds on poor little Tracy. The smaller man would never stand a chance.

The volume of Eli's growl grew steadily louder and more menacing. Tracy looked to him for aid, but Kellan felt no pity for the man. Tracy had crossed a line and gotten himself into this mess—he would have to get himself out of it. When Tracy realized Kellan was not going to come to his aide, his brows furrowed and he glowered at Eli. Rising to his feet, he slowly made his way to the door. With a hand on the doorframe and his chin high, he turned to Kellan.

"You obviously need time to think things through. I'll call you in a couple of days, when you've had time to get your priorities straight and have kicked the riffraff to the curb." Tracy's mouth curled into a sneer as his gaze flicked over Eli.

Eli's body visibly tensed, the muscles and veins of his arms straining against his skin, his fists clenched so tight they were nearly white against his skin's normal olive hue. When Eli took an angry step forward, Tracy bolted out of the room so fast Kellan could have sworn he left a vapor trail behind. Flinging open the door, he practically ran down Jai, Dylan and the rest of Kellan's Betas who had apparently heard Eli growling and come to save the day. Kellan tried to stifle his laughter as Jai entered the room, watching Eli warily.

"You all right there, E?" Jai asked, concern heavy in his voice.

Kellan watched Eli blink slowly as if waking from a dream. He looked around, bewilderment clear on his face. "What happened?" he asked hesitantly.

"Oh, nothing really," Jai drawled, sarcastically. "I mean, besides the fact that you just went all rabid dog on Tracy, nothing at all."

For a moment, Eli's expression was awash with confusion. Then, suddenly, that lack of understanding transformed into a look of pure horror, which then finally morphed into intense fury. The emotions were changing so fast, Kellan was having a hard time keeping up. The constant changing was so comical, Kellan had to fight back a laugh. When those blue eyes turned on him, rage burning in their depths, Kellan had a feeling the situation was about to get a whole lot less funny.

"You son of a bitch!" While the yelling was definitely a surprise, the large fist flying at his face was so unexpected, Kellan barely had time to rise from his seat and prepare for the hit. He was able to turn enough that the incoming fist slammed into his cheek instead of the eye it had been aiming for. The pain was incredible. Black spots bloomed before his eyes and it was all he could do to keep on his feet. Gritting his teeth kept him from shouting out, but just barely, as he waited for the pain to reach a bearable level.

"What the fuck, E?"

"Don't *'What the fuck, E?'* me, asshole! What the hell do you think you're doing, kissing me when you're involved with someone?" Chest heaving, Eli's body was nearly vibrating with rage, his black eyes sparking with fury.

Kellan was so turned on, he nearly missed what Eli was saying. "Wait... What? Involved with someone? What the hell are you talking about? The only person I'm involved with is you." Kellan was genuinely puzzled. Eli was his mate. There was no way he could be involved with someone else. He took a step closer, wanting to comfort his mate, only to be forcefully shoved back by the smaller man. However, even in his anger, Kellan could tell Eli held back. With his shifter strength, he would have been able to throw Kellan across the room if he'd wanted to. No matter what he said or did now, Eli definitely cared for him, at least enough to temper his anger and keep from causing him any serious harm.

"Don't give me that bullshit, Kellan. When we walked in here, you had the redhead practically riding your cock for the whole club to see. Then, not five minutes ago, he's climbing all over you like he's a stripper and you're his pole. How does that not translate to you being involved with someone?"

Eli was talking about Tracy? Kellan and Tracy hadn't been dating, and they definitely hadn't been exclusive. They'd just been having fun. They had just been passing the time until one, or both, of them met their mate. When Kellan had found Eli, his arrangement with Tracy had ceased to exist. Didn't his mate understand that? And how could Eli's lips look so amazing when he was scowling so viciously at him? It made him want to kiss his mate until the expression cleared.

Kellan leaned closer to Eli, entranced by the sight of his full bottom lip. The stormy look in his dark, bedroom eyes slammed into Kellan like a punch to the chest. Without a thought, Kellan reached out to brush his thumb gently across that plump bottom lip. When he pushed just the tip inside his mouth, Eli went so still, Kellan wasn't even sure he was still breathing, his eyes impossibly wide. "Such a gorgeous mouth," Kellan murmured to himself. "So beautiful. I can't wait to see it stretched tight around my cock."

Eli gasped before jerking back violently. Panic and anger filled his eyes. "What the fuck, Kellan?"

Realizing what he'd just let slip out, Kellan raised a hand, desperate to calm his skittish mate. "Calm down, baby. There's nothing to get worked up about. Why don't you take a seat and we can talk about things, okay?" Kellan soothed.

Eli's eyes narrowed as he took a step back. "Fuck you, Kellan! I'm not your baby. I'm not your anything." Turning his back on the Alpha, Eli made his way over to Jai. "I'm sorry, Jai. I can't deal with this right now. My wolf's too close."

Jai flashed him a concerned smile. "Of course, bro. No worries. Do you need me to come with you?"

"I'll be fine on my own." Eli gave him a sly, slightly strained smile. "Why don't you stay and blow off some steam before you come home?"

Jai laughed. "I think I might just do that. Thanks, man!"

"Stay safe and don't do anything I wouldn't do. I'll see ya later at home."

Kellan watched helplessly as Eli gave his friend a quick clap on the back and turned on his heel. He was out of the back entrance of the club before Kellan even had the chance to wish him a good night. Dropping into his chair, he lowered his head, resting it on the desk.

"Fuck!!" he roared, furious with himself. He slammed his fist onto the table top.

Dropping down onto the couch, Jai leaned back and casually took a pull from his beer. He smiled cheekily, looking on as his Alpha had his breakdown.

"Well, Kellan, I've got to say, that could definitely have gone better."

Chapter Three

Ever since he was a kid, Eli had always worked through his issues by punishing his body. For some indefinable reason, working out always brought him clarity. It helped him narrow his focus, which, in turn, helped him to better see the big picture. With clarity being something he was in desperate need of, Eli was thankful that the whole basement level of Jai's building had been converted into a gym.

When Jai showed up hours later, Eli was working the heavy bag, hard. Wearing only black gym shorts, running shoes and athletic tape securing his hands, he was dripping with sweat and his hand wraps were stained pink with blood. The sound of flesh impacting echoed off the walls in a steady rhythm, like the beat of a drum, driving him on.

Jai, ever the considerate friend, noisily entered the room, letting Eli know without words that he was no longer alone. As he approached, Eli stopped attacking the bag, bending to grab the bottle near his feet before pausing to drink deeply. He grabbed a towel off the floor and was wiping down the bag when Jai reached him.

"Do you want to talk about it?"

Eli appreciated the fact that Jai knew him well enough not to push and make everything a big deal. He had never been receptive to that approach. Running fingers through his sweat-slick hair, Eli let out a breath, trying to find the right words. In the end, he opted to go with honesty. "I don't know, man. I've been down here for hours and I still can't wrap my head around it."

Jai tilted his head, thoughtfully. "What's got you twisting in the wind on this, E? Is it because Kellan kissed you? I know Kellan is really sorry he lost control of himself at the club. He's worried that he pushed you too hard, and now you'll never give him a chance."

Eli let out a surprised laugh. "No, Jai. Surprisingly, the kiss isn't freaking me out like I thought it would. I mean, yeah, I've never been attracted to a guy before and I just made out with one in a room full of people… But it was…okay. It was strange, but it was also kinda nice. The way I felt when Kellan kissed me… I've never felt that way before with any of the women I've slept with. It's weird, but I'm dealing with it. I don't know where I stand in the gay-straight-bi argument, but at the moment, I'm okay."

He hoped Jai would hear the truth in his words and stop worrying so much. He was worried his friend would misunderstand his conflict with Kellan and assume it was an issue with him being gay. That couldn't be further from the truth. Thankfully, judging by the look of relief on Jai's face, he understood what Eli was trying to get across.

"Then what's up with the workout marathon?" Jai tilted his head to the side, his voice soft and coaxing. From his wrinkled brow to pursed lip, concern was clearly written across Jai's face. Unfortunately, his question rekindled the anger that Eli had spent the last few hours trying to control. A growl worked its way past his teeth before he could bite it back, eliciting a look of shock from Jai.

"I'm pissed, okay?" Eli snarled as he began to pace, agitation building within him. He could sense the subtle shift of his eyes, showing how close his wolf was to the surface. His time without a pack, combined with his anger, was pushing him dangerously close to losing control. Eli had always been the even-tempered peacekeeper of the Steele family. He had never been so close to losing himself completely to his wolf. Though he would never admit it to anyone, he was scared.

"I don't understand," Jai replied soothingly. "If you're not mad about the kiss, then what's the problem?"

Throwing down his towel, Eli whipped around to face Jai. "That son of a bitch came on to me...kissed me...while he was involved with someone else. That's not the kind of man I am, Jai. I won't play the whore for Kellan-fucking-Reeves!" Hurt and vulnerability were clear in his voice, and in the moment, Eli hated himself for his weakness. The confusion brought on by having feelings for another man was hard enough to handle. The fact that he had let Kellan hurt him with his cold and callous behavior was inexcusable. He had been born a Beta, for Christ's sake! He was supposed to be stronger than this.

"E," Jai murmured cautiously, "Kellan is not dating Tracy. He and Tracy have had a mutual hook-up arrangement for the past few months. It was basically a 'friends with benefits' kind of deal. They weren't even exclusive. To be honest, I'm pretty sure Tracy would fuck anything that moves." Reaching out, Jai placed a soothing hand on Eli's arm. "You know me, E. If he was a cheating scumbag, you know there is no way I'd cover for him. Trust me."

Eli tried to hold onto his anger. It was easier to focus on that than try to understand the other emotions churning inside him. While he didn't regret the kiss, he was still trying to come to grips with what it meant in the grand scheme of things. If he could just stay angry, he could put off having to deal with the huge changes that were happening in his life. The open, honest expression on Jai's face, however, punched holes in his resolve. As a result, he felt hope start to build in his chest, burning away his doubts.

Eli took a breath. "Okay."

"Okay?" Jai raised his brow. "Just okay?"

Eli gave a half-hearted imitation of a smile. "Yeah...for now." Wrapping his towel around his neck, Eli threw his bottle in the recycle bin and headed for the door.

They made their way back down the hall to the elevator in silence. Eli still couldn't believe he had basically let Kellan dry hump him in the middle of the dance floor. Not only had he allowed him to do it, but Eli had truly gotten into it. He couldn't remember the last time he had gotten that hot, that fast. The knowledge that it had happened with a man had definitely shocked him. Never in his life had he ever had any doubts about his orientation. While he'd never had any problem recognizing that another man was good-looking, he'd never felt even the slightest attraction to another man. Not until Kellan Reeves.

Now, as he was assaulted by a multitude of new feelings and emotions, all he had were doubts.

As the doors closed them in, Jai cleared his throat. "So, you and Kellan, huh?"

Out of the corner of his eye, Eli could see the smirk on his friend's face. "Drop it, Jai," Eli groused.

The silence between them was brief. "Does this mean you're gay now?" Jai asked, false innocence dripping from every word.

Eli could hear the amusement in his friend's voice and fought back the urge to give him a head slap. "God, you are such a dick," Eli muttered, shaking his head.

"Hey! Just because you're gay now, doesn't mean I want you to be thinking about my dick, ya perv!" The mock outrage in Jai's voice was too much for Eli to handle with a straight face. The laughter that followed seemed to loosen the knot that had been tightening in his chest the last few hours. Jai's laughter joined with his own until they were gasping for breath, tears rolling down their faces.

"You are such a prick," Eli accused, when they'd gotten themselves under control.

Jai laughed. "Listen to you. You've been gay for all of like five minutes and now all you can think about is cock."

The punch to Jai's arm came swift and hard, but did nothing to stop Jai's laughter. They were both still chuckling as they exited the elevator and made their way back to Jai's apartment. Once inside, Eli threw his towel in the hamper before heading to the kitchen to get a glass of water.

"I talked to Kellan before I left the club tonight. We set up a meeting for later in the week, if that's still all right with you?" Jai let the announcement hang in the air between them.

Just the mention of the Alpha's name had Eli's pulse racing at breakneck speeds. He nodded his acceptance, thankful his friend had still had the presence of mind to remember why they had gone to the club in the first place. "Thanks, man. I appreciate all your help with this."

"Are you kidding? You're my best friend and I need you here. I've missed you these last few months." Jai stopped, looking slightly uncomfortable. "You know Kellan is going to want to know what happened, right? Even if he wasn't interested in a relationship with you, he would want to know what would cause a strong Beta wolf to leave his familial pack where he would have become Second to the Alpha."

"I know."

"What are you going to tell him?"

"The only thing I can tell him—the truth." Eli released a weary sigh. "If he's willing to let me join his pack then, as my Alpha, he has a right to know. I just don't want my being here to cause any problems for him or the pack. He has enough to deal with without having to worry about trouble from my past."

"I don't think you have anything to worry about." Jai placed a reassuring hand on his shoulder. "If he gives you a hard time, you can always shove your tongue down his throat again to convince him to let you join the pack."

Jai's attempt to lighten the mood fell flat at the reminder of what had happened between Eli and the Alpha. Eli's jaw clenched as he ran a shaky hand through his hair.

"Does this mean I'm gay, Jai?" Eli asked softly, surprised by how broken his words sounded. While he had always been completely accepting of Jai's orientation, the possibility of his own homosexuality had knocked him off his axis and into a new world, filled with possibilities he knew nothing about and didn't understand. If what was happening between Kellan and himself was real, he had no idea how to deal with it, or what was expected of him.

Jai gave Eli a wistful smile. "I wish I had an answer for you, E. It could mean nothing. It could mean everything. Being attracted to one guy doesn't necessarily make you gay. It could mean that maybe you're Bi. It could mean that you're just curious. One moment of attraction doesn't mean you have to go buy a rainbow sticker for your truck, start marching in parades and change your whole life."

Eli tilted his head to the side. "What if I want it to mean something? I can't deny what I felt when Kellan kissed me. I don't think I would want to deny it, even if I could."

Jai flashed his friend a reassuring smile. "I think you have the time to figure it out. Nothing has to be decided tonight. I know Kellan. He cares for you and he will give you all the time in the world, if you need it, for the chance that you might feel the same. I definitely wouldn't start losing my mind over it yet." Jai gave him a sly smile. "I mean, honestly, how much more can you afford to lose? Before long, I'll be changing your diapers and trying to stop you from talking to inanimate objects."

A ghost of a smile twitched on Eli's lips. "Oh, come on, Jai. You'd use any excuse to get a look at what I'm packing."

Jai returned the smile. "Oh, so you've finally caught on to my evil plan?" He rose from his seat and turned toward the hall. "Well, since you seem to be adjusting fairly well, I'm gonna go crash. After watching all your drama unfold, I feel like I'm ready to pass out. I'll see ya in the morning, 'kay?"

"All right, see ya in the morning... And, Jai?"

Jai stopped his progress down the hallway and turned to face Eli. "Yeah?"

Eli smiled, gently. "Thanks, man. You know...for everything."

Jai winked. "No worries, E. Occasionally I have to use my superpowers for good." Hips swaying saucily, he made his way down the hall to his room, closing the door quietly a minute later.

Eli shook his head in amusement before shutting off the lights and heading for his own bed. He needed to get some sleep. He had a lot of work ahead of him if he was going to make a new life in Grand Rapids. He only hoped that whatever was going on between he and the Alpha wouldn't keep him from being accepted into the pack. He didn't want to worry Jai, but he could already feel himself slipping. Too long without a pack, and a shifter would go feral. The more powerful the wolf, the faster it happened. Eli had walked away from his pack two weeks ago. At the rate it was progressing, he wouldn't make it another two. If he couldn't get Kellan to accept him into the pack, chances were good he would have to be put down.

Chapter Four

Days passed, without as much as a word from Eli. If it hadn't been for Jai calling to keep him updated, Kellan would have gone out of his mind. He was trying to be understanding, but with his wolf pushing him to claim their mate, it was getting harder and harder.

From the news he'd been getting from Jai, the two men had been busy getting Eli settled into his new life in Grand Rapids. The first issue they had tackled was Eli's business. According to Jai, Eli had started his company, Steele Security, when he had returned home from his final tour in the Marines, three years earlier. When he renounced his old pack, he had left his brothers—Noah, Micah and Reid—in charge of the Mason Valley location. Since Grand Rapids would be his new home, he was planning on making it the new headquarters for the company. Eli and Jai had been out scouting locations and had signed the lease on the perfect building just that morning.

Jai had been excited when he'd called with an update, claiming that the site was huge and would fit their needs perfectly. The main floor of the facility would house the business and technical side of the company and the lower level provided room for training and housing personnel, if needed. With the new location, Eli was planning to expand the business into providing and training bodyguards, as well as the state-of-the-art security systems his company was already known for.

While Kellan was excited for his mate, he was also becoming more and more annoyed with his continued silence. While he appreciated the updates from Jai, Eli should have been the one telling him about his company and the new building. This was the kind of thing that mates shared with each other. The fact that they needed an intermediary was starting to seriously get on Kellan's nerves. Thankfully, the day of their meeting had finally come. If his mate did not show up for this, Kellan was going to hunt him down and bite his delectable ass.

Kellan was in his office, drowning in paperwork, when he sensed his mate's arrival. Throughout the day, he had been able to pick up a slight hint of nervousness through their barely formed link. Now, with his mate in the same building, he could feel his normally calm mate coming down with a massive case of nerves.

Peeking into his mate's thoughts, Kellan chuckled softly to himself, amused by the fact that his wayward mate thought that he might be punished for his behavior of the last few days. While Kellan might not like their separation, he understood Eli's need for it. His mate had needed space to examine the situation and make an informed decision. Kellan understood that his mate would always be the type to look at all facets of a situation before rushing to judgment. That quality in itself made him the perfect mate for an Alpha.

A knock on his door pulled him from his thoughts. Kellan called out for them to enter before pretending to focus on his paperwork. Jai and Eli were ushered to a set of chairs opposite Kellan's massive desk, while Dylan and a few additional Betas found seats throughout the room. It was customary for Betas to sit in on Admittance Determinations, either to welcome the new member of the pack or to make sure the rejected applicant didn't decide to answer the Alpha's decision with violence. The room was silent as Eli and Jai waited for Kellan to acknowledge them and begin the meeting.

Kellan took a moment to get his thoughts in order before setting aside his paperwork and turning his attention to the men who sat before him. When he looked up, he only had eyes for Eli. His mate's eyes had gone nearly black with need and he knew an answering hunger must be reflected in his own emerald orbs. The kiss they had shared, just days ago, had started a fire building inside him. The desire to claim his mate was now a living, breathing thing that took all his strength to fight. With the heat building between them with just a look, Kellan couldn't begin to imagine how explosive it would be when something more physical happened. They would probably set the room ablaze.

Neither man was willing to look away. They continued to basically eye fuck each other until someone strategically cleared their throat, interrupting the moment and bringing both men's attention back to the room. Kellan growled his displeasure at the interruption, before turning his attention back to the matter at hand.

"Elijah Matthew Steele, previously of the Mason Pack, I welcome you. Jaimeson Nicolas Miller, Gamma of the Grand Rapids Pack, you are welcome here." His tone was all business and resonated with the power of an Alpha behind it. With a brief nod of acknowledgment to his Betas, his shoulders relaxed and he pushed the offending papers off to the side of his desk, clearing off the center as he leaned forward to address them. "Now that we've got the formalities out of the way, Jai, in what capacity are you here today?"

"First and foremost, I am here to support my friend. I'm also here as a character witness, if one is needed."

Kellan's brows furrowed in response. "You think I would make him provide character witnesses? You should know better than anyone that this meeting is just a formality. As far as I'm concerned, he is already a member of this pack."

When Jai merely shrugged, Kellan's scowl deepened. Turning away from his annoying friend, Kellan turned his attention back to his mate. Nerves had obviously gotten the best of him if the bouncing of his leg was any indication. Kellan would have laughed if he didn't think the man was clinging to the edge by the skin of his teeth. "Eli, we're here to address your recent application to join the Grand Rapids Pack as a permanent member. Looking at the petition, I see that it says that you are requesting admittance as a Standard wolf. Is this correct?"

The sound of Jai's sharply indrawn breath of surprise echoed in the room as Kellan watched his mate's expression. Apparently, Eli hadn't told his friend about his application for Standard status.

"Yes, Alpha. That is correct."

"You were born a Beta in your birth pack. Second only to the Alpha, from what I've been told. Why the hell would you want to go from being at the top of the pack hierarchy, to being just one of the regular masses?"

Eli's eyes clouded and the look of betrayal that flashed across his face tore into Kellan. His mate looked like the walking wounded. Kellan wanted to comfort the smaller man, but the expression was gone as quickly as it had appeared. Eli's shoulders drooped, leaving his arms to hang limply at his sides. His expression changed, becoming so empty of emotion that Kellan felt his heart clench.

Eli cleared his throat. "I found that as Beta I was expected to follow some orders that were directly against my beliefs and values. It was for that reason I renounced my birth pack. As a Standard, I would be just another member of the pack. While I would still be expected to follow orders, the chance of getting many direct orders from those in authority would be much smaller. An Alpha's time is spent mainly with the Betas and Gammas of the pack. A Standard wolf is left to his own devises, as long as he keeps his nose clean and stays out of trouble. All I want is to be able to start a new life, led by my own choices."

The question Kellan was so desperate for the answer to was, of course, the one his mate didn't want to answer. He didn't want to force his mate to give him the information, but he knew anything less than an order would be ignored by the stubborn man. "No more beating around the bush, Eli. Tell me what happened."

Eli ran a hand through his hair in agitation. "My father is Charles Steele, Alpha of the Mason Pack. He's always been an asshole and a terrible Alpha. He's abusive and intolerant of anyone he sees as different. The only reason I stayed with the pack after Jai left was to help protect the weaker members until the time my older brother, Noah, took over as Alpha. Noah is everything my father is not. He has a good heart and will be an amazing leader."

The smile that flickered on Eli's face told Kellan how much his mate cared for his brother. Being an only child, whose parents had passed away many years before, Kellan had always longed to have a family. The love his mate felt for his brother made Kellan yearn to inspire that kind of devotion in his mate, as well. Regretfully, they would need to get through this period of acceptance and adjustment before he could hope to have the kind of relationship he yearned for with his mate.

"Eli…" Kellan urged, when his mate continued to hesitate. "Please, continue."

Eli's jaw clenched. "Fine. My father tried to force me into an arranged marriage with a fifteen-year-old girl. He tried to claim it was for 'the good of the Pack'. He said that in order for us to stay strong as a species, we had to increase our numbers, breeding new, strong members for the Pack." Disgust colored Eli's words. "When I told him I couldn't see how mating with a child could possibly strengthen the Pack, he laughed in my face and told me that that was because I had no vision."

Kellan stiffened, his body rigid, as he tried to make sense of what Eli was saying. "How could he think of doing that to a child, let alone his own son? Surely the girl and her family had objections to this?"

Eli's mouth twisted, a sad imitation of his usually luminous smile. "Just the opposite. Her family was new to the Mason Pack and saw our mating as a chance at power and prestige, elevating them in the eyes of the Pack and raising them quickly through Pack hierarchy. The girl saw me as a trophy and she used the possibility of our mating as a way of ostracizing the other single women in the pack. She believed her being chosen proved her superiority and used that belief to ridicule and torment other members of the Pack. Don't waste your pity on her, Kellan," Eli said, flatly. "She was no innocent."

Kellan shook his head, his thoughts running in a million different directions. "But why a girl so young? Why open himself up to that kind of scrutiny? Surely other members of the Pack took issue with her age, if nothing else. Why not choose a Pack member closer to your own age?"

Eli shrugged. "The girl's father owns some kind of biochemical engineering company outside of Detroit. For some reason, my father was desperate to have them join the Pack. There were rumors that our mating was part of my father's negotiation to convince them to stay. Obviously," Eli muttered dryly, "it must have worked."

Kellan struggled to process the information Eli had given him. The only thing that truly made any sense to him was Eli, and how close he had come to losing him. A growl rolled out of his chest and echoed off the walls until the room was filled with the sounds of anger and pain. It only grew louder and more menacing as he focused on what his mate had told him and what it would have meant for the two of them. Kellan could feel his wolf trying to force its way out, but he was past the point of caring. The beast within him shared his rage. Both he and his wolf understood that if those people from Eli's past had had their way, their mate could have been married off to someone else — lost to them forever. The rage building within him seemed to suck all the oxygen out of the room, leaving many of his Betas gasping for breath, as he was overwhelmed by the red tide of fury encompassing him.

"Did he succeed, Eli?" Kellan snarled, more wolf than man.

"Did who succeed, Kel?" Eli responded, cautiously.

"Alpha Steele. Did he succeed in forcing you to claim another? Did he force you to sleep with her?" Not waiting for an answer, Kellan leaped over the desk, wrapped a hand around Eli's throat and pulled him in close. His mate cried out, but it did not deter him. He had to be sure. He had to know that no one had tried to claim what rightfully belonged to him. In some of the oldest packs, there were stories of matings being forced through subversion and magic. Kellan knew the odds of that happening were slim, but he wasn't willing to take any chances. Not with his fated mate. Burying his face in Eli's neck, he dragged in a deep breath, immersing himself in the scent that was completely Eli. A second breath confirmed the first — his mate had not been forced to accept another.

The relief that filled him was nearly overwhelming. To think he had come so close to losing his mate, before he'd even known he existed. The thought rekindled the fire that had been burning within him all week. The urge to claim his mate, to keep anyone else from taking what was his, was beyond his strength to fight. His wolf needed release, demanding they claim their mate. Torn between his own needs, and the desire to wait for his mate to be ready, he felt like he was literally being torn in half. In a moment of desperation, he called out for the one thing he knew would bring him peace.

"Eli!"

Chapter Five

"Everyone, out!" Eli's authoritative voice boomed through the room, shocking everyone and sending them into a flurry of motion.

"Eli, what do you think you're doing?" Dylan demanded, his brows furrowed and eyes dark as pitch.

"He's not going to hurt me, Dylan. I am his mate and he needs me. You guys need to get out of here."

"This isn't a good idea, Eli. Please...reconsider." Worry lined the Beta's face, but Eli didn't have time to reassure him. His main concern was the man before him who was struggling to maintain control, despite the demands of his wolf. Eli could sense Kellan's control was slipping and wasn't sure how much longer he would be able to hold on.

"Eli is his mate. He would never do anything to hurt Eli." Jai's voice was calm and sure as he tried to pull Dylan from the room.

"Damn it, Jai! Think about what you're suggesting. Even if Eli's willing, he has no experience with a male lover. Kellan won't be able to do sweet and gentle.

How the fuck do you think Kellan will live with himself if he knows he's responsible for damaging his mate?"

Eli met Dylan's eyes, begging him to understand. "I'm strong, Dylan. I can handle whatever he dishes out."

Sadness and resignation crept into Dylan's features as he backed out of the door. He looked over at his snarling, snapping Alpha then back to Eli. "Yeah... You can handle it, but will you be able to forgive him for it?" Without another word, he gave a shout and led the rest of the men out of the room.

As Jai turned to leave, Eli felt the first real bite of apprehension. "Jai. Any advice?"

"Lube," Jai replied, his voice wavering slightly as he, too, backed into the hall. "Lots and lots of lube."

Eli choked out a laugh, feeling the tension within him ease just a bit, as the door clicked shut softly behind his friend. Turning to face the man who claimed to be his mate, he hoped like hell he had made the right decision.

Kellan was a fearsome sight to behold with his green eyes flashing and chest heaving. His long hair was free from its usual queue and fell down to his shoulders. A tick had formed in his jaw and Eli found himself entranced by the flexing muscle. Even in a state of such extreme anger, he couldn't help but be drawn to the powerful man before him. He was drawn to Kellan by a force stronger than anything he'd ever felt before. Even now, with Kellan on the verge of a total loss of control, Eli still wanted him. That knowledge was like sunshine clearing away the fog of doubt in his mind. Eli was Kellan's mate and it was time for him to start acting like it.

Eli straightened and fought the urge to take a step back. Instinctively he knew that now was not a time to show weakness. He kept his eyes focused on a point just over Kellan's shoulder, so as not to be interpreted as a challenge.

"Kellan?" When he got no response, Eli took a chance and glanced at Kellan's face. His eyes were narrowed and held a dangerous glint of fire in their depths. His arms were held stiffly at his sides and his hands were clenched so tight, the knuckles had gone white. Eli tried to swallow around the lump in his throat but was having a hard time now that nerves had taken hold of him.

"Kellan," he repeated, louder. He could tell the bigger man was fighting an internal battle with his wolf. Eli needed to know what he could do to help Kellan win that fight.

"I didn't want it to happen like this…" Kellan growled. "I didn't want to force you to be with me. I wanted to wait until you were ready… When you wanted it too…"

"I do want you, Kellan. It just took me a little while to figure it out."

Again, he received no response. Eli was still trying to find the right words to reassure the bigger man when Kellan closed the distance between them in three large steps. He wrapped one massive hand around the back of Eli's neck, thrust the other into his dark locks and crushed their lips together in a punishing kiss. Eli was so surprised by the suddenness of Kellan's actions, he was left momentarily unable to react, until a threatening growl rumbled from Kellan. Obviously, Kellan meant for him to participate. Eli's lust-fogged brain was quick to get with the program.

The first, tentative flick of his tongue was a bit awkward, but when Kellan started to suck his tongue, Eli lost all his reservations and forged ahead, unrestrained. Under their own direction, his arms wrapped around Kellan's waist, pulling their bodies flush against each other. The hard ridge of Kellan's shaft dug into Eli's abdomen, as Eli's own erection rubbed shamelessly against Kellan's thigh. He ground their groins together, trying to get enough friction to push himself over the edge.

With a menacing growl, Kellan broke the kiss, ripping off his own shirt before shredding Eli's as well. Advancing, he shoved Eli roughly against the wall before continuing his carnal assault. He licked and nipped his way down Eli's neck and jaw. Thrusting his thigh between Eli's legs, Kellan allowed him to rub against him like a bitch in heat.

A growl rumbled from Kellan's chest as he panted against Eli's lips. Eli swore it was the most erotic sound he had ever heard. Surrendering to his wolf's instincts, he let his head fall back and rode Kellan's heavy thigh with abandon, losing himself in a pleasure more intense than anything he'd ever experienced before.

Eli whimpered when Kellan's hands released his head, only to moan throatily when he felt the same hands shift into claws and attack the button and zipper of his pants. His cock was so hard it felt like the denim of his pants had it in a stranglehold. Then, with a pop and a hiss and a draft of cool air, he was free. Kellan jerked his jeans and boxer briefs down to his knees in seconds. The predatory smile that crossed his face as he took in his first glimpse of Eli's naked body had Eli praying that he had made the right choice.

Chapter Six

"Fuck, yeah," Kellan groaned as he stared at his mate's obscenely engorged shaft. "You are so damn perfect." Eli was sporting what had to be at least nine inches of uncut, drool-inducing perfection between his thighs. His sac hung heavy and swollen, just begging for attention. His long, thick shaft was dripping pre-cum like a leaky faucet. Kellan moaned as he gave in to the temptation.

The shock on Eli's face when Kellan dropped to his knees in front of him was priceless. Kellan shoved his face into Eli's sac and inhaled, taking in the intoxicating, musky scent of his mate. The scent helped calm the frenzy still burning inside of him. He rolled his eyes up to Eli, flashed him a grin and swallowed his cock down to the root.

Kellan watched his mate fall apart. Alternating between soft, teasing licks and suction so strong it would have made vacuum manufacturers proud, he was desperate to drive his mate out of his mind. Grabbing Eli's hips, he jerked him forward, encouraging his mate to fuck his mouth.

Eli faltered as if unsure how to proceed. When the first few thrusts were delivered, they were shallow and hesitant. Kellan snarled in outrage. He was no swooning woman wanting to be treated with kid gloves and soft words. He was the Alpha!

"Fuck my mouth, Eli! Now!"

Eli's eyes widened briefly, and Kellan watched as his mate's whole body shuttered at the order. Reaching down a hand, his mate slowly ran his fingers through Kellan's hair before gripping it tightly in his fist. Eli grabbed his cock in his free hand and brought it up to Kellan's parted lips. Assuming he was about to get his favorite treat back, Kellan was surprised when Eli slapped his thick shaft against his cheek.

Looking up to meet his mate's gaze, what Kellan saw there had his heart pounding in his chest. A fire was burning behind those black orbs and Eli's expression was fierce. Twice more Eli's cock slapped against his skin before it was shoved back into Kellan's waiting mouth.

No longer holding back, Eli repeatedly snapped his hips forward, driving his shaft farther and farther down Kellan's throat. Kellan gloried in his mate's loss of control as he held Eli's ass cheeks in a bruising grip. Reaching down with one hand, Kellan toyed with his mate's heavy sac, rolling and yanking on the hefty orbs. Kellan felt Eli's balls tighten minutes later, signaling his impending climax. Eli urgently shoved at Kellan's shoulder in warning, but Kellan merely shrugged him off, not wanting anything to distract him from the reward he was about to receive.

"Gonna come..." Eli moaned, barely getting the warning out.

Kellan pulled off his cock in a slow glide, flicking his tongue over the head as it popped out of his mouth. The smile on his face was just plain wicked.

"That's the plan, baby. You're gonna fuck my mouth, hard and fast. You're gonna shoot that huge load down my throat. Then, when I'm done sucking down every drop of spunk you've got to give, I'm gonna bend you over my desk and eat your ass till you scream my name."

Kellan watched Eli's face for signs of panic, now that he knew some of what Kellan had planned for him. With his lips bruised and pupils blown, he looked gloriously debauched. Finding nothing but lust in his mate's midnight gaze, he attacked Eli's cock with a renewed urgency. He loved the feel of the satin-covered steel sliding in and out of his swollen lips. He licked, flicked and laved his mate's big cock to within an inch of its life. Pulling back slightly, he teased the gland under the head before starting to tongue fuck the weeping slit. Eli cried out and his sac pulled up tight.

Sensing his mate had reached his limit, Kellan reached between Eli's legs and started gently massaging his perineum. By the second pass of his fingers over the sensitive skin, Eli was shooting like a rocket down his throat and Kellan was drinking it down like a starving man. Damn, he tasted fantastic! Kellan sucked greedily, like he was drinking the finest wine. He gently massaged Eli's balls, milking every drop from his sac before licking him clean and rising to his feet.

Looking down at his mate, Kellan's heart seized at the sight before him. Eli's breath was coming in heavy pants as he lay half sprawled across the corner of Kellan's desk. His normally pale skin was flushed a gorgeous shade of pink and small droplets of sweat gave it a slight sheen. Eli looked thoroughly ravaged, but Kellan was nowhere near done with him.

Leaning over his mate, Kellan pressed against him as he crushed their mouths together in a brutal meeting of tongues, lips and teeth. With the remnants of Eli's release still on his tongue, Kellan shared the flavor with his mate who moaned desperately in response. He allowed Eli to suck his tongue until the last remnants of his release were gone. Pulling back from the kiss, Kellan's smile was all teeth.

"You liked that, didn't you, baby? Loved the way it felt with my mouth so hot and tight around your cock, huh?"

The groan he received in response sent his blood boiling through his veins. Damn, he needed to be inside Eli more than he needed air to breathe. He knew he didn't have much time before he spilled his seed on the floor, instead of deep inside his mate. Desire for his mate coursed through him with an intensity he had never felt before. Eli was nearly ready for him, but Kellan wanted him so far lost in his lust that he wouldn't even be able to think about refusing him. He wanted Eli so turned on he'd be begging Kellan to fuck him.

Gripping Eli's hips, Kellan roughly spun him around, shoving him face first down over the side of his desk. When Eli tried to push himself up, Kellan put a firm, restraining hand between his shoulder blades.

"Stay still!" he snarled. "You don't make a move without your Alpha's permission. Do you understand?"

Eyes wide, Eli gave a jerky nod in response. Mesmerized by the sight before him, Kellan trailed a large, warm hand down the slope of his mate's back and over the firm mounds of his ass. Palming the muscled globes, Kellan gently spread them to reveal the most perfect pink pucker he had ever seen. He wanted to taste it—needed to taste it.

Leaning forward, Kellan blew a steady stream of warm air over his mate's twitching hole. Eli jolted like he had been electrocuted and Kellan smiled. This was going to be so much fun. Moving in, he licked a slow line up Eli's crack, causing Eli to cry out in surprise. God, he tasted amazing! Delving back in, Kellan fluttered his tongue around the outside edge before forcing it through the tight outer ring to get a taste of the man beneath him.

A strangled moan tore from Eli's throat. Fucking perfect! Kellan loved how responsive Eli was, loved that he wasn't able to hold back any of his reactions. As Kellan bathed his hole in hot, wet heat, Eli rocked back against his face to meet every probing lick of his tongue. While he was lost in the pleasure of it, Kellan gently eased a thick finger inside him. Eli gave no indication of discomfort when Kellan pushed deeper. When his finger brushed against his prostate, Eli howled out a curse.

"Fuck! Kellan...what are you...?"

"Easy. Just relax and let me in, E. Gonna make you feel so good."

Much to Kellan's excitement, Eli immediately obeyed his order. Eli was beautiful in his submission and Kellan couldn't help but be grateful for it. As Alpha, he was born with the need to dominate, needing to receive submission in return. Eli's natural acceptance of the submissive role helped settle his wolf. Thankfully, with his wolf's desperation no longer driving him, Kellan was able to regain a modicum of control. It served to remind him that, until Eli became used to the more intimate nature of their mating, he would need a softer touch. With his finger still buried in his mate's ass, Kellan began a slow thrusting rhythm, fucking Eli gently with his finger as he worked to loosen his virgin muscle. Eli was hesitant at first, but when Kellan started hitting his gland with every thrust, pleasure took over and Eli became lost in the sensation. He started rocking back into the thrusts, forcing Kellan's finger deeper and harder into his grasping hole. Instinct had Kellan carefully adding a second finger as his thrusts became quicker and harder. Scissoring them apart, he stretched Eli's hole before quickly pushing in a third.

Moans and curses were streaming steadily from Eli's mouth as he thrust back, over and over again, onto Kellan's thick digits. When Kellan reached around and started pumping his cock, their volume increased.

"That's right, baby. Fuck yourself on my fingers. Ride 'em hard. Show me how much you like it."

"Kellan," Eli gasped. "I…n-need… I need…"

Kellan leaned over his back, his hot breath tickling Eli's ear. "What do you need, E? All you have to do is tell me, and it's yours."

"I… I need more…Kel…"

"What do you need more of, E? Do you want more fingers fucking you? More of my tongue in you, eating your sweet hole? Or is there something else you want? Maybe you want something bigger in your ass, hmm? Is that it, E? You want something bigger in you?"

"Yeah…bigger, Kel. Something bigger, something more." He shoved himself back, violently, on Kellan's thrusting digits. Just watching him, Kellan could tell that Eli had given himself over to the pleasure and need building within him.

"Tell me, E," Kellan growled, fiercely. "Say the words and I promise I will give you everything you want." Grabbing a handful of Eli's hair, Kellan jerked Eli up, slamming their bodies together. "Say the fucking words, baby!"

"Your cock, Kellan!" Eli cried. "I want your cock. Please, fuck me!" Eli was practically screaming.

"Ahh, now that's what I wanted to hear. Anything you want, E. Anytime, anywhere. All you ever have to do is tell me."

Kellan jerked his fingers from Eli's ass, eliciting a groan from the smaller man, and ripped open the front of his own pants. When his cock made its appearance, Eli blanched and paled. He was only slightly longer than Eli, but considerably wider. While Kellan could understand Eli's trepidation at taking Kellan's big cock into his virgin ass, it wouldn't change anything and they both knew it. Both Kellan, and his wolf, needed release.

"I don't know about this, Kel." Eli's eyes were huge as stared at his heavy dick. "It's so damn big... I don't think..."

"Trust me, Eli. It'll fit and once I get it all crammed up in there, you're gonna feel so fuckin' full. You're gonna love it. Your ass was made for my cock." Reaching into his desk drawer, Kellan pulled out a bottle of lube. Since discovering Eli as his mate, he had been hiding the stuff everywhere. Dylan had told him it was just wishful thinking. Now, Kellan couldn't be more grateful he hadn't listened to his friend.

Pushing his jeans down his thighs, he slicked up his cock, root to tip. When he came back to Eli, he could tell his mate's nerves were getting the best of him by the tension in his shoulders and back. He ran a soothing hand down his spine while reaching around with the other to jerk Eli's beautiful cock. The moan that fell from Eli's lips nearly made Kellan give up his load right on the spot. Fuck, this man got to him. He tightened his grip on his mate's thick shaft as he positioned his own at Eli's entrance.

"Now, you gotta relax for me, baby. It's gonna burn at first so you've just got to breathe through it. Because once I'm in there, bottomed out, balls deep in your ass, it's gonna feel so good, you're never gonna want me out. Gonna ride your ass so hard, you'll be feeling me there for weeks, and you're gonna love every second of it, aren't you? Tell me, baby. Tell me how much you want it." He licked up the side of Eli's neck and snagged his earlobe between his teeth. Eli shuddered and thrust his hips back, letting Kellan's dick ride the crack of his ass. Kellan draped his big body over Eli's back. "Tell me," he whispered.

"I want it, Kel," Eli moaned, still pumping his hips, fucking air. "I want you to fuck me. I want you to ride me, your monster dick in my ass, stretching me wide. Please, Kel. I need it, now."

Just that fast, playtime was over. Kellan took the time to smear a bit of extra slick over Eli's hole, lined up his cock and pushed. With Eli being a virgin, logic told him he had to take it slow, but with E whining and wriggling under him, he just couldn't help himself. He'd gotten about halfway in when Eli's ass contracted around his cock like a vice, then suddenly holding back was no longer an option. His control snapped and he thrust forward, bottoming out hard.

Eli and Kellan groaned in unison. Eli's ass was so tight it felt like it was cutting off circulation to his dick every time it squeezed around him. It felt so good and Kellan wanted to move so badly, he felt like his head was gonna explode, and not in a good way. "E, baby, tell me I can move. Fuck, I have to move, please!"

A soft chuckle resonated out of Eli's chest before working its way through Kellan by way of their connection. Kellan groaned as he pinched the base of his dick to stave off the climax that was trying to finish things before they even began. He popped Eli hard on his right ass cheek and the moan the man let free nearly killed Kellan.

"Like that do ya?" Kellan could see them having a lot of fun with his mate's little spanking kink. He could already picture Eli draped over his knee, naked ass in the air, turning cherry red under Kellan's ministrations.

"Fuck, yeah. Come on, Kel. Are we gonna talk all night or are you gonna fuck me through the floor? You can't leave me like this, I'll die. Finish it." Desperation was clear in Eli's voice. His mate was in need.

That was all the incentive Kellan needed. He thrust home with brutal force, releasing his control, and began pounding into Eli. "Christ, E, you're so fuckin' tight. Hot and tight and squeezing my dick so good. I think I just want to spend the rest of my life inside you. Never wanna stop fucking you. You're so damn perfect!"

"Might...make it hard...finding pants..." Eli gasped.

Kellan snarled. "If you can still make jokes, I'm obviously not fucking you hard enough." Kellan punctuated the statement with a thrust Eli could probably feel in his throat. The sound of skin slapping echoed in the room around them. Kellan grasped Eli's hip with one hand while he twined the other in his mate's inky locks, yanking his head back, smashing their lips together in a devouring kiss. Eli moaned when Kellan released his hair to grab his other hip. With a firm hold, Kellan thrust into Eli with everything he had, jerking him back onto his cock, trying to get as deep into his man as he possibly could. He wanted to crawl right into his skin. His balls tightened as they slapped against Eli's ass, his climax approaching quicker than he would have liked. Eli just felt too good. There was no way to slow things down, not this time.

"That's it baby. I'm so close and you're gonna come with me, aren't you? You ready to fly, E?"

"So close, Kellan. I have to come. Please, let me come."

"Not yet! You don't come until I say, you understand, E? You will wait until I give you permission, won't you? You're gonna listen to your Alpha, baby, aren't you?"

"Oh, God," Eli groaned. "Please, please, please..." He chanted the mantra over and over.

Kellan waited until he felt his own climax reach the boiling point, before shouting out. "Now, Eli! You shoot now, with me, or you don't get to finish at all. Come, baby!"

Chapter Seven

Boy, did he ever. As soon as the words were spoken, Eli was shooting like he had never shot before. He came so hard it felt like he was turned inside out. His balls ached, his cock throbbed and his ass heated as Kellan filled him with his release. Eli collapsed, no longer able to hold himself up. All his strength had abandoned him in the face of that kind of passion.

Closing his eyes, Eli took a minute to enjoy the feeling of floating that accompanied his climax. A sense of joy and peace settled over him, comforting him like a warm blanket on a cold day. It felt like all the pieces of his life had been forced to fit into spots they didn't belong and it had taken Kellan to step in, tear the puzzle apart and start over to get them all to fit the right way. It was a scary feeling.

Mate, Kellan had called him, right before their encounter. Eli had never honestly thought about taking a mate, male or female. It was terrifying how much he was thinking about it now…wanting it now…with this man.

The strength of his desire was something he had never experienced before. It was exhilarating, but it also left him feeling like he was standing in a burning building and any minute the floor could cave in and he would be devoured by the flames. He didn't think he would be able to handle losing Kellan. Not now, after the major eye opening he'd just experienced. He had to know if Kellan was serious about being mates and where the big man saw this heading.

"Why didn't you give me the bite?" The question nagged at Eli, making him wonder whether Kellan truly believed they were destined mates, or not.

Kellan smiled, leaning in to place a gentle kiss at the corner of Eli's passion bruised lips. "I wanted to wait until we were both in our right minds, making a choice that would set the stage for the rest of our lives. Bad enough that you had to experience your first time with a man while I was half out of my mind. When you are ready to accept me as your mate, I want there to be no doubt in your mind that you are making the right choice."

A smile tugged at his lips and heat coursed through his body at Kellan's heartfelt words. He couldn't have imagined more perfect words to set his mind at ease. Suddenly uncomfortable with his silly, sentimental thoughts, Eli squirmed under Kellan's heavy weight until the big man surrendered his position and lifted himself off Eli's back. Finally, he could breathe again. Eli pulled himself to his feet and immediately regretted it. The room started to spin and his legs threatened to give way beneath him. Thankfully, Kellan still had the presence of mind to lunge for him when his legs buckled, and kept him from crashing to the floor.

"Whoa," Eli stammered, slightly dazed. "That's never happened before."

Kellan flashed one of his cocky smiles. "I will take that as a compliment, my mate." Concern eclipsed his smile as he observed Eli. "You okay, E?"

The mate comment helped to clear some of the fuzz from Eli's brain. He knew they had to address what had just happened and what it meant for the two of them. "Yeah, I'm good. Kel, I..."

Just as he was about to voice his concerns, Eli's cell started chiming from somewhere in the room. A chagrined smile crossed his face as he looked around and took in the destruction they had caused in their haste. Chairs were flipped over, papers were strewn around the room and Kellan's massive desk had moved about five feet from its normal location. Their clothes were everywhere. It looked like someone had ransacked the room. What a mess.

It took the two men nearly fifteen minutes to locate all their clothes and set the room to rights. It would probably have taken less time if they had been able to stop touching and kissing each other. The weirdness of being intimate with a man was definitely a thing of the past for Eli.

When Eli finally retrieved his phone from under the desk, he saw that he had three missed calls, all from his older brother, Noah. *Strange*. While the brothers had always been close, it wasn't normal for Noah to call three times in the span of an hour. Especially since they hadn't spoken at all since the day Eli walked away from his familial pack, weeks ago. Something had to be wrong. Quickly accessing his messages, he skipped right to the last message in his mailbox.

E, it's Noah. I'm on my way to Grand Rapids. I need to see you as soon as possible. Call me as soon as you get this message...and be careful.

Eli just stared at the phone in his hand with a puzzled expression for a moment, before he jolted into action. If Noah was calling to give him warnings, something serious was going on. He pressed the button to dial Noah, holding up a finger at Kellan's questioning gaze. Noah answered before the phone had even finished its first ring. *Weird.*

"Hey, Noah, it's Eli. What's up?"

"E, thank God! I've got to see you. Something really screwed up is going on with the Pack. We need to talk."

Eli scoffed at the obliviousness of his statement. "Yeah, Noah. Something is definitely screwed up with the Pack. Our father tried to force me to marry a child and start breeding the next generation of pure-blood Shifters, or don't you remember? Why the hell should I care? It's not my pack anymore, so I could really give a shit!"

For a moment, there was silence over the line. "What do you mean, not your pack anymore, E?" Noah asked, quietly. "You're my Beta. Once we get all this shit straightened out, you're coming back to help me run things."

"Screw you, Noah. Were you not at the same meeting I was, where our father tried to force me into marrying a minor? I wasn't trying to make the meeting a little more exciting and add to the drama factor when I renounced the Pack. I'm done with it. I'm a member of the Grand Rapids Pack now and I have to say," Eli announced, glancing slyly over at

Kellan who was watching him with a curious expression, "I've never been happier."

The look of satisfaction on Kellan's face served to reassure him that he had made the right decision in accepting what was between them, despite his reservations. Just looking at the man was getting him worked up again. When his thoughts turned to dropping the phone and seeing how fast he and Kellan could get back out of their clothes, he knew he had to get his mind out of the gutter and back on track.

"So, Noah," he drawled, a wicked edge in his voice, "has father set you up with your own blushing bride, yet? I bet he can't wait until you join the ranks and help him start breeding his future army." Yeah, Eli was still irritated with his brother for his lack of support when he walked away from the pack and he was letting it show. Eli could admit that he and maturity were not always on speaking terms.

"Christ, E! Could you just shut the fuck up for like, two seconds?" Noah let out a sigh that was almost completely drowned out by the growl released by Kellan. With superior shifter hearing, Kellan would have been able to hear both sides of the conversation as if it were happening in that very room. Apparently, he was taking exception with the attitude Noah was aiming at Eli. Call him childish, but it made Eli want to cackle with glee.

"All right, Noah, I'm listening. What's going on?"

"I don't want to get into it over the phone." He hesitated. "You really joined another pack, E?" The words were said so quietly, Eli almost missed them. His strong, Alpha brother sounded so lost. For a second, he almost felt bad for leaving him the way he had, but it only took another moment for him to remember why he had. Eli's remorse vanished quickly.

"Yeah, Noah," he confirmed. "I really joined the pack here and I'm happy with my decision. This place...it feels like home." The look on Kellan's face warmed Eli's heart. His smile could have lit the whole world.

It was quiet on the line for long enough that Eli worried his brother may have disconnected the call. He was just about to hang up the phone when Noah spoke, his voice cool and distant. "I'm on my way to you and Jai's place, now. I should be there within an hour. Bring your Alpha if he's free. From what I hear, he's a good man and I could use all the advice I can get right now."

The hard edge to his voice was something Eli had never heard before. It helped clear Eli's mind of any residual anger or resentment. Noah was worried about something and it took a lot to rattle his older brother. "What's going on, Noah? You have to tell me something. If you want my Alpha there, I'm going to have to give him some kind of information."

His brother sighed. "Tell your Alpha that I believe we have a coup being planned in Mason. Warn him that I believe his pack may be on a list of packs marked for attack and takeover. Things have been weird back home for a while, E. You being set up to marry that girl was not a coincidence. There is a reason Dad was so keen to have that family join the pack. I'm tellin' ya, something very messed up is going on."

Eli couldn't believe what he was hearing. The Mason Pack had been peaceful for as long as he could remember. Even when learning about pack history, he had never heard of any instance where their pack had instigated a fight with another pack. It was incomprehensible. He glanced over at Kellan. His mate's eyes had narrowed, dangerously.

"I'll pass on your message and ask if he has time to meet with you. He's recently found his mate so I'm not completely sure if he will be available." Eli looked over at his mate, a small smile appearing on his lips. The big man just shook his head, chuckling softly. Noah's voice brought him back to the conversation.

"All right, well, anything you can do to get him to meet with me, I would appreciate. I know as a new pack member, sometimes you don't have a lot of pull with the hierarchy. If he screws with you, you give him my number and I'll set him straight."

Too late, Eli thought sardonically, thinking of his tender ass. "I don't think that will be necessary, Noah, but I'll keep it in mind. I'll speak with the Alpha and then head over to the apartment. See ya in a bit, okay?"

Noah released a breath, in relief. "Sounds good, E. I'll see ya in a few. And thanks, again."

Chapter Eight

Kellan looked on as Eli ended the call. After what he had just heard, his thoughts were a jumbled mess, leaving him unable to focus. When Eli slowly approached, Kellan reached out and wrapped the smaller man in his strong arms, pulling him tight into his body. The comfort he got from the embrace and the scent of his mate immediately soothed some of the agitation of his wolf.

"Well," Eli murmured, giving Kellan a quick kiss under the chin before pulling away and starting toward the door, "I'm gonna head over to the apartment to wait for Noah. Why don't you round up your Betas, give them an update then meet me over there?"

"Excuse me?" Kellan snarled, deciding he must be having a problem with his hearing, because nothing people were saying today made any sense. Looking down at his mate, Kellan's jaw clenched at the expression of expectation on his face. "You have got to be kidding me. I must have fucked all the brains out of your head, if you really think I'm going to let my mate leave here, alone, to meet with the heir apparent of a rival pack that, we've just learned, is planning to invade my territory."

The fierce growl emanating from him echoed through the room like thunder, but Kellan was past caring. He was not going to let his mate be hurt by anything, least of all his own bad choices. "You go nowhere alone! If I am unable to accompany you, you will take one of my Betas for protection, but you do not go anywhere by yourself, starting now. I will not have an enemy pack abducting my mate. I will not lose you!"

Eli stared at him in silence. With his wide eyes, furrowed brow and hands clenched tight at his sides, it was obvious Kellan's mate was not happy with his order. No matter, he could handle it. Kellan was willing to suffer far more than the Eli's wrath, if it meant keeping his mate safe and whole. However, the longer the silence stretched, the more nervous Kellan became. He saw something flash in Eli's eyes, before he took an aggressive step toward Kellan.

"I think you may be confused about who I am, so just this once, I'm gonna cut you some slack. However, the next time you decide to go all 'caveman' on me, I will kick you in the balls so hard, you'll need testicular retrieval surgery if you ever want to see them again. I am the second-born son of an Alpha and a born Beta. I served in the Marines for five years and when I came home, I used the security training I had received to start, and successfully maintain, my own private security firm."

"I'll tell you who you are," Kellan interrupted, snarling. "You are my goddamn mate! Mine to love and mine to protect. Mine!"

"I don't need your protection!" Eli countered. "I am not weak, I am not your wife and I am not like those boys that your circle likes to keep around. I do not need you to protect me or keep me safe. I do a damn fine job of taking care of myself and those around me. If you are looking for someone to cower behind you and make you feel big and strong, you've got the wrong guy. I will fight beside you or I will fight without you. Wrap your mind around it. Take all the time you need. I'm sure I wasn't what you were expecting to get in the mate department. Who knows? Maybe you've just got a bad case of lust and the whole 'mate' thing was a mistake. I'm giving you the opportunity to walk away, no hard feelings."

Eli's words hit Kellan like a brick to the chest. The implications of what he said were soul shattering. He met his mate's gaze with eyes gone flat and cold. "And could you, Eli?" The question was barely more than a whisper but filled with anger and pain. "Would you be able to just walk away from what's between us?" Kellan knew that if this man tried to walk away from him, it would probably kill him. Death at that point would be a mercy. He didn't want to live in a world where Eli Steele wasn't at his side. He was willing to do anything to make his mate happy... Anything, but risk his life in a fool's mission.

Sadness crept into his mate's midnight gaze, and his eyes took on a wet cast. "If that was your wish, I would do anything necessary to make you happy."

Eli's simple words froze Kellan in place. How could his mate ever think he would wish him gone? Didn't he understand that Kellan loved him more than his own life...more than his pack...more than being an Alpha?

Eli used his moment of distraction to make his way to the door. Kellan could only look on as his mate moved with strong, confident steps. He swung open the door and stepped into the hall, before turning to meet Kellan's troubled gaze. "You know where I live. Let me know when you've decided what type of mate you want."

With his parting words still hanging between them, he closed the door gently behind him, leaving Kellan alone in the quiet of the empty room. He stared at the closed door, silently fuming. How dare Eli give him an ultimatum? He was the Alpha and, as such, it was his responsibility to protect his mate, not the other way around. The fact that Eli didn't understand that made Kellan further wonder why the gods had chosen to give him a mate so different from his usual type. His past lovers had always been quick to follow his lead, allowing him his dominant role both in and out of the bedroom. While Eli didn't seem to have a problem submitting to him between the sheets, his incessant demands to stand shoulder to shoulder with Kellan when it came to outside issues were cause for concern. How could he protect a mate who was dead set on putting himself in harm's way? Was it so wrong for Kellan to want to protect the most important person in his world? The one man who gave his life meaning? Kellan hadn't thought so. At least not until his mate had walked out of his office…possibly for good, if Kellan couldn't find some middle ground where both of them were happy.

A knock at the door pulled his mind away from thoughts of his wayward mate. He called out a greeting and the door opened, revealing a slightly concerned Dylan. His Beta entered the office and approached him. By the expression on his normally stoic face, Kellan knew he had something to say but was struggling to find the words. Kellan didn't have the time or inclination to wait for him to mince words.

"If you've got something to say, just say it."

"Is Eli all right?" Dylan's words were cautious.

"Of course, he's okay," Kellan snarled. "He was well enough to hand out orders and ultimatums before he stormed out of here to go play hero."

"I'm sorry, what?"

Kellan quickly gave Dylan a rundown of the altercation with Eli and his mate's subsequent exodus from the building. His anger flared as he recounted his mate's complete disregard for his Alpha status. When Dylan turned fierce eyes on Kellan, he was sure that his Beta understood his ire and was angry on his behalf.

"Permission to speak freely," Dylan growled.

"Of course," Kellan answered smugly.

"You are an idiot."

Kellan stared at his friend in disbelief. "Excuse me?"

"I'm sorry. Would you like me to speak slower?" Dylan quirked a brow. "You have been gifted by the gods with a kind, compassionate, strong mate. You should be down on your knees, thanking them for that gift. Instead, you have driven him away with your selfish need to always be in control."

"I am an Alpha," Kellan stammered, taken aback by his friend's vehement, verbal smack down.

"That is no excuse for how you have treated your mate. Yes, you are an Alpha, but did you ever take even a second to consider the fact that your mate is a Beta? He was born with the instinct to protect others. Would you have him ignore part of who he is, all so you can prove that you are a big, strong Alpha?"

"Well... I..." Kellan struggled to find words to defend himself.

"No," Dylan interrupted, "of course, you didn't. As you said — you are an Alpha. Why would you deign to consider anyone's nature but your own? Look at the changes Eli made in order to accept that you were his mate." Dylan met Kellan's gaze, his eyes suspiciously shiny. "If I had a mate who agreed to be mine, I would do everything in my power to keep them and make them happy. Are you truly telling me that you are not willing to do the same?"

Dylan didn't bother waiting for an answer. Shaking his head in disgust, he turned on his heel, threw open the door and marched out of the room without as much as a backward glance. Kellan stared after him in shock. As Dylan's words sank in, he had a moment of doubt. Was it really possible that he was the problem in this equation? Kellan rejected the thought immediately. No. This was Eli's problem and it would be up to Eli to fix it. It was as simple as that. For now, any further reflection on his relationship with his mate was going to have to wait. They had bigger problems to deal with.

At the moment, he knew he needed to get his Betas and Gammas together and update them on the situation. Once they were up to speed, they would handle getting the word out to the rest of the pack. The pack needed to be notified of the possible threat, and everyone needed to be alert to anything suspicious or out of place. It was their best chance of heading this thing off, with the least amount of damage to his pack. He had a responsibility to the people who followed him so, for now, while their safety was in question, they had to be his top priority.

Once the word got out, and people were prepared and at the ready, he would be able to go to his mate and work things out. Grabbing his cell phone off the desk, he made his way out of the club. He quickly placed calls to his Betas and Gammas, updating them on the situation and giving out orders to bulk up their defenses. He was finishing his last round of calls as he reached the parking lot. Jumping into his truck, he headed downtown, hoping to make it to Jai's apartment not long after Eli. Even with his pack on alert, Kellan didn't like the idea of his mate being on his own, unprotected. The sooner he got to the apartment, the sooner he could work on fixing things with his mate.

Chapter Nine

Eli had only been home for a few minutes when his phone rang. A quick check of the screen told him it was Noah, probably to give him a heads-up on his proximity to the apartment. "Hey, bro. You almost here?"

A dark chuckle sounded over the line. "I'm sorry. Noah seems to have run into some car trouble. It doesn't look like he's going to be able to make it. Perhaps I can come and fill in for him?" The threat in the voice was undeniable, causing the hair on the back of Eli's neck to rise.

"Who the fuck is this? Where is my brother?" Eli fought to keep his voice calm. *Fuck*! What the hell had happened to Noah?

"Eli, it hurts that you don't recognize me. After all the quality time we've spent together, getting you ready to take over Beta position? I guess I thought I'd be memorable."

"What the fuck! Carl? What the hell have you done with Noah?" Carl Yager was one of his father's Betas. He, as well as his father's other Beta, Mario Costa, had been working to train him, over the past few years, to take over the duties of a Beta wolf. Eli had never liked Carl, but he never would have thought he would do something crazy like harm the future Alpha. Carl had to have lost his mind.

"Now, now, Eli. No need to get worked up. I haven't done anything to Noah he won't be able to recover from and nothing that wasn't approved by my Alpha. Seems Noah was getting a little too big for his britches. He decided to start talking about things that were none of his business. Alpha Steele decided Noah needed a little quality family time back home. You know, time to get his head on straight and be reminded what's really important in life—family, loyalty, Pack. You know what I'm talking about, Eli? We're thinking you could use a little reminder, as well."

Eli's blood ran cold. Could they be coming for him, too? He tried to slow down his thumping heart and calm his breathing. He listened for any sounds that were out of place—a creaking floorboard, a thump against the wall or a whispered breath. Quietly he waited, hearing nothing. When Eli was convinced he was truly alone, he turned his attention back to the conversation.

"See, Carl, that's where the problem lies. I'm not a member of Alpha Steele's pack anymore, so even if he wanted to remind me of what's important, he no longer has the right. Any punishments for me, at this time, would be handed out by my new pack leader, Alpha Kellan Reeves. Any grievances Alpha Steele has with my behavior would have to be brought to Alpha Reeves, to handle as he sees fit."

"Eli, Eli, Eli," Carl chastised. "You and I both know you're going to be the Beta of the Mason Pack. There's no way you would join another pack and be just another peon. It's time for you to come home and face your punishment, Eli. Come willingly and I promise, no harm will come to you...well, at least not right away." Carl's deep chuckle caused Eli to shiver. There was something seriously wrong with Carl Yager, and his own father for that matter. What did these men think they were up to?

"Carl, I'm completely serious when I tell you that I am no longer a member of the Mason Pack. Ask my father. When I renounced the Pack the day I left home, he felt my connection to the Pack break. Whatever he's told you is a lie, Carl. I don't belong to him anymore. I belong to Alpha Reeves, now."

Eli knew he had to try something to get through to Carl. So far nothing else he had said seemed to work. "Carl," he said, trying to sound as sympathetic was possible. "If you come here and try to take me, my Alpha will be furious. He will come after you and he will hurt you. I don't want you to get hurt over a misunderstanding between me and my father. You're a good man, Carl. I would feel awful if you got hurt over this." Eli held his breath, hoping he had gotten through to Carl.

Unfortunately, Carl seemed completely oblivious to Eli's words. "I can't wait till you're back home where you belong," Carl growled. "I spoke with your father about us."

Us? Eli ran the statement over in his head. There was never, and would never be, anything between him and Carl. He could barely tolerate the man and until that very moment would have been sure the other man disliked him as well.

"He promised me," Carl went on, unaware of Eli's confusion. "He promised that after you mate that

Tremmel girl and get a pup bred on her, you'll be mine. I've waited so long, Eli. Now, soon, we'll be together and everything will be perfect."

What the fuck? His father was going to give him to Carl, as well as Meloni Tremmel, his would-be child bride? He couldn't even fathom what had led his father to do this. Again, he tried to appeal to Carl.

"Carl, what about Laura? What about your wife? You love her and she would be devastated if you left her for me. You don't want to do that to her, do you? It would break her heart. And what about your children, Carl? They would never understand. Things like that aren't done in the Mason Pack, Carl. Alpha Steele doesn't not condone same-sex matings. It is forbidden. Remember what the pack did to Jai? You don't want that for yourself, do you, Carl?"

"No, Eli, you don't have to worry. Your father promised he would allow it, as long as you breed a pup on the girl first. All you have to do is knock her up and you're mine. I have such plans for that body of yours..." Carl sounded so intent...and completely insane. Somehow, his father's Beta had become completely disconnected from reality. Eli didn't trust the look in the other man's eyes. They had taken on a slightly sadistic gleam. He had seen a similar expression on Carl's face in the past...whenever he had been ordered to deal out a particularly brutal punishment to a Pack member who had displeased Eli's father. Eli knew, then, that there would be no reasoning with him. Eli had to switch tactics.

"Carl," Eli implored, "I can't even think about going back to Mason until I can see Noah. I have to make sure he's all right before I leave. Is he still with you or is he already on his way back to the Pack?"

Eli prayed that Carl had been sent alone. If Carl was there by himself, there was a chance he could get Noah back while he still had the home court advantage. If Noah was already being transported back to Mason, he would have to take on the whole pack to get him back. That would absolutely suck, and not in a good way.

"Noah's still with me, Eli. We were waiting on you. Noah is very anxious to go home, Eli. I can tell, just looking at him, how sorry he is for disappointing your father. Alpha Steele is going to be so happy to have his family back together. I can't wait to tell him."

Eli practically cheered out loud. Now this could work in his favor. All he needed to do was get Carl to come to him and bring Noah with him. He momentarily thought about pulling it off on his own, but after brief consideration he knew it was a better idea to call Kellan to get back-up. He'd never forgive himself if something happened to Noah because he was too stubborn to ask for help. He drew out his silence, hoping to convince Carl he was truly considering going back to Mason. After a moment, he let loose a deep sigh of resignation.

"All right, Carl, you're right. I need to go back to Mason and try to fix things with my father. I hate the strain this has caused on my family. I miss my brothers, the Pack, everything. I'm not making any promises that everything is going to work out right away, but I am willing to try. Is that okay, Carl?"

"Aww, see, that's all I'm askin' for. Just give the old man a chance. You'll see. We just have to get through this whole mating deal and knocking the bitch up, and then you and me can be together, just like we should be. Everything's gonna be perfect, Eli. You'll see."

The almost domestic words coming from such a disturbed person were nearly more than Eli could take. The thought of Noah being anywhere near the troubled man set Eli's teeth on edge. He knew he had to keep up the act, if only to buy them more time. Noah's life depended on it.

"Now, Carl," Eli murmured softly, "I need to know how Noah is. I won't be angry with you. I know whatever you did to him was because he disobeyed my father and my father required you to discipline him. My only concern is making sure he really is going to recover completely. I hate to think what would happen to you if Noah was worse off than you thought and he didn't make it. My father's anger would be unstoppable. I can't let him hurt you, Carl. Please, tell me about Noah?"

Carl's hesitation confirmed Eli's suspicion that things with Noah were considerably worse than he had led Eli to believe. Carl mumbled to himself for a moment before turning cold eyes on Eli, a slight smirk twisting the corner of his lips.

"He's really messed up, Eli. I worked him over real good, just like your father told me to. He's kinda out of it right now, but I don't want to talk about him anymore. What I want to talk about is all the plans I have for that virgin ass of yours."

"Carl," Eli said softly as he fought back a shiver of revulsion, "I need you to bring Noah to my apartment. Jai's out for the night and won't be home for hours so you don't have to worry about seeing him. I need to check Noah out to make sure he is going to heal properly. I have all the supplies I need here. Can you do that for me, Carl? Please? Once I know he's okay, we'll have all the time in the world to talk about your ideas."

"All right, Eli. I'll bring Noah to you. I'll load him back into the van and will be there in about an hour. Get your supplies ready and pack up all your stuff while you're waiting so we can hit the road when you're done fixing him up. Your father wants us back home as soon as possible. Full moon is Saturday and he wants everything on schedule for the marriage ceremony. I'm leaving now. I'll see you soon."

Chapter Ten

Kellan barged into the apartment just in time to witness Eli drop the phone and take off running to the bathroom. The initial anger he had felt from what he had overheard of the phone call quickly vanished under the immediate concern he felt for his mate. Quickly following Eli's path down the hall, Kellan found his mate hunched over the toilet, losing the contents of his stomach into the porcelain throne. He crouched down on the floor, rubbing gentle circles across Eli's back, and whispering soothing words in his ear.

They stayed there, hunched together on the cold bathroom floor, for what seemed like hours. Moisture beaded on Eli's forehead as his stomach continued to rebel, even after there was nothing left to eject. Thankfully, the tremors began to ease, leaving Eli wrung out and weary on the bathroom floor.

Grabbing a towel from a cabinet, Kellan turned to the sink and wet it, before kneeling next to his mate, gently mopping the sweat from Eli's brow and neck. When he finally got a look at his mate's face, he couldn't ignore the red-rimmed eyes and wet cheeks. Cupping Eli's face in his hands, Kellan forced Eli to look at him. "Who was on the phone, E?"

When Eli refused to answer, Kellan tightened his grip, forcing him to give Kellan his undivided attention. "I don't care who the hell he is, E. I will kill him if he thinks he's going to take you from me! You are mine! Your place is at my side, and I don't care if you hate me for it. I will love you enough for the both of us."

For a moment, Eli just sat there on the floor, staring at Kellan silently. Kellan was starting to worry that there was something seriously wrong with his mate, when he finally broke his silence.

"He hurt Noah," Eli murmured, his voice barely more than a whisper. "He's on his way here. I told him I had to make sure Noah doesn't die."

"Your brother Noah?" Kellan asked, trying to make sense of Eli's disjointed ramblings. "Who hurt your brother, E? Tell me what's happened." Though the words were spoken quietly, the order in them was unmistakable.

The order from his Alpha seemed to ground him, cutting through the haze and confusion that had paralyzed him. He seemed to snap out of his funk, right before Kellan's eyes. Quickly, Kellan was given a rundown of his mate's 'chat' with a man named Carl Yager, as well as a description of what had been done to Noah. With every word Eli uttered, Kellan's anger grew. When Eli finished his explanation, Kellan instantly sprang into action, calling his Betas and directing them to get to the apartment as fast as possible. He overheard Eli pick up his own phone, calling Jai to warn him away from the apartment until things had calmed down. Kellan barely hid his laughter when he overheard Jai, ever so politely, tell his mate to "Get fucked!" and that he would be at the apartment within ten minutes. Smiling to himself, he couldn't believe how grateful he was that Eli had had a friend like Jai in his life all these years.

After placing a few additional calls, organizing pack members and handing out orders, Kellan ended his call, before shoving his phone back in his jacket pocket. Turning, he found Eli watching him, lust and something indefinable shining in his eyes. The combination immediately made him hard. Christ! The man could turn him on just by breathing. He watched as Eli's breath came faster, until he was almost panting. It was nice to know he wasn't the only one affected. He took a step closer, noticing the way Eli's pupils dilated. Damn, he wanted to fuck him again. If only there was time.

Closing the distance between them in two large steps, he wrapped a large hand around the back of Eli's neck, pulling him into his body. The heat rolling off him soaked into Kellan, warming him thoroughly. Leaning forward, Kellan nibbled along Eli's full bottom lip before drawing it into his mouth. The desperate moan that fell from his mate's lips only served to amp Kellan's need. Shoving a heavy thigh between Eli's legs, he silently directed him to spread them. Eli complied, giving Kellan more room to accommodate his larger body between his thighs. Encouraged by his actions, Kellan began to thrust against Eli's groin, grinding their cocks together in a rhythm that was just short of maddening.

Eli spread his legs farther as Kellan lifted him, allowing him to ride Kellan's muscled thigh. Desperation bloomed in Eli's eyes as he fought to get more contact. Reaching between them, Eli frantically tore at the closure of Kellan's jeans. His hands were quickly bracketed and forcibly stilled by Kellan's thick, meaty hands. Eli met Kellan's gaze, a question burning in his stormy eyes.

"I want you," Kellan reassured his mate, "but we don't have the time. My people will be showing up here any minute and we have to be ready for Carl when he gets here. While I'd like nothing better than to bend you over the counter and make a meal of your ass, we've both got to calm down. I promise, after we catch this crazy fuck, you will spend the next week riding my cock, but for now, we have work to do."

Kellan watched as Eli's eyes glazed and he let out a shaky breath. "Saying shit like that does nothing to help calm me down, Kel." His mate glared up at him, bringing a smile to his lips. Kellan watched as Eli struggled to beat down his raging libido. The whimper that escaped his mate was music to Kellan's ears. The scent of Eli's arousal was thick in the air causing Kellan's nostrils to flare and his eyes to narrow as his own need burst back to life, even stronger than before. Eli was visibly holding his breath, waiting for direction from his Alpha.

The wait didn't last long. Kellan lunged at Eli, dragged him into the kitchen and shoved him, face first, onto the counter top. Kellan didn't even give his mate a chance to take a breath before he had Eli's pants around his ankles and Kellan was on his knees, prying his ass cheeks apart. A puff of warm air was all the warning Eli received before Kellan attacked his asshole. Long, wet licks were followed by sharp nips and a fluttering tongue around his hole. Eli gasped for air, begging incoherently. Kellan burrowed his tongue into Eli's cleft, desperate to get a taste of his mate's most intimate spot. When his tongue breached Eli's tight ring, Kellan swore he had found heaven. The teasing licks quickly evolved into forceful thrusts as that talented tongue tried to reach new depths within his mate. Forging his tongue inside as far as he could, Kellan then did a slow drag back out, while simultaneously sucking hard on his mate's sweet hole. Eli was above him on the counter, moaning like a bitch in heat, shoving his ass back into Kellan, riding his thick tongue.

Kellan grasped Eli's ass cheeks in a firm grip, shoving both of his thumbs inside, and opening him wide. His perfect, pink hole was twitching and winking, just begging to be filled. Kellan, mind lost to lust, was determined to answer its demand. He pulled back, admiring the view of his mate, open and vulnerable before him,

"Look at you," Kellan growled. "Ass wide open for me. Your hole twitchin', just begging me to fill it up. You are such a slut for my cock, aren't you, E? Tell me what you want. Beg me for it."

Eli moaned, a broken, desperate sound. He arched his back, trying to force Kellan's monster prick into his hungry hole. Kellan pinned him to the counter and gave his ass a hard slap. Eli groaned, going limp in his arms.

"Oh, you definitely like that. That is something we are going to explore in great detail, in the very near future," Kellan murmured, softly in his ear. "If we had more time, I would make you wait for my cock until you begged me. Unfortunately, the rest of the guys will be here any minute and I have to get inside that ass." He pushed two meaty fingers into Eli's mouth, coating them with his saliva before shoving them into his hole. "I don't have any lube, so we are going to have to make this work."

Without warning, Kellan removed his fingers and thrust forward, burying his thick cock in Eli's tight chute. He didn't stop until he bottomed out, balls resting hot against Eli's ass. They moaned in unison while they became accustomed to the sensation. After a moment's pause, Kellan reared up, thrust a hand in Eli's hair and jerked him back, flush against his body. With a tight grip on his hip, Kellan began thrusting roughly into Eli's eager hole.

"Christ, you feel good. There's no better feeling than my cock in your ass, riding you hard and deep. Tell me how much you love riding my cock, E."

"Fuck!" Eli thrashed in his arms, and Kellan was loving every second of it. "Dammit, Kel! Feels so good. So full... So hot... Never want you to stop. Fuck me, Kellan! Don't hold back. Give it to me now!"

Kellan roared. His control snapped as he began hammering into Eli with everything he had. Eli arched his back, meeting Kellan thrust for thrust. Releasing his hip, Kellan wrapped his hot hand around Eli's leaking prick, jerking it roughly. He felt Eli's sac pull tight, signaling his impending release. Leaning forward, he licked Eli's lobe before snagging it between his teeth.

"I'm so close, baby," he groaned. "I'm about to pump your tight ass full of spunk. When that happens, you better be shootin' too. I want to see you spray those cabinets white with your cream, you understand me?"

Another sharp slap was delivered to Eli's ass, making him moan. Eli jerked his head, showing Kellan he understood. After a handful of thrusts, Kellan felt a telltale shiver roll through him, alerting him that release was eminent. He snapped his hips even harder against Eli's backside, fighting to hold off just a second longer.

"Now, Eli!" Kellan roared as he emptied his seed into Eli's hot channel. It felt like he came for hours. Jerking his hips as he continued to pump his release into his mate's willing body, he could feel his cum overflowing Eli's chute and coating his inner thighs. He shot so long and so hard, his dick actually hurt when he ran dry.

The scorching heat of Kellan's cum filling his mate had the desire effect, bringing Eli into a screaming orgasm of his own. As Eli fell over the edge, Kellan let his canines extend before plunging them into his mate's vulnerable throat, claiming him in a way both wolf and man demanded. Kellan needed everyone to know that this man belonged to him and that no one would ever take what was his. While the wound would fade over time, the scar it left behind would be visible to anyone who dared to get too close to his mate.

As the sweet taste of his mate's blood coated his tongue, Kellan's dick jerked in a valiant attempt to release more of his seed into his mate. His bite seemed to intensify Eli's pleasure, if his moaning and thrashing was any indication. Kellan could sense his initial shock being chased away, as the pain of the bite quickly morphed into an even more intense wave of pleasure. Over and over, Eli came, dousing the cabinet in front of him with a thick cream coating.

Hunched over Eli's prone form, Kellan was filled with a smug satisfaction as he gently eased himself free of his mate's still fluttering hole. Eli whimpered but did not attempt to rise as Kellan left him and made his way down the hall to the bathroom. He returned moments later with a warm washcloth, then proceeded to wipe down every inch of his mate's beautifully exposed skin. Leaning forward to kiss the back of his mate's neck, Kellan smiled when Eli released a satisfied sigh.

Once finished, he threw the soiled cloth into the bathroom before making a quick stop at the fridge to grab a couple of bottles of water. Eli pushed himself off the counter and back on his feet as Kellan handed one of the bottles to him, before quickly finishing his own.

Closing his eyes, he was attempting to bask in the afterglow of an amazing fuck when he felt his mate's scrutiny. Opening one eye, he scowled at the gorgeous man. "Something I can help you with, E?"

Eli sighed wearily, running agitated fingers through his raven locks. He paced the room like a caged wolf before rounding on Kellan. "I don't know what the hell is going on with me. I can't believe I just begged you to fuck me on my best friend's kitchen counter while my brother may be dying and in the hands of a psycho." He shook his head in disgust. "What the fuck is wrong with my head?"

Kellan's heart went out to Eli. He knew the whole situation had to be totally screwing with him. He was actually surprised the man had been handling all the recent changes so well. Going to his mate, Kellan pulled Eli into his arms, and embraced him tightly.

"There's nothing wrong with you, E. What we are feeling is completely natural and totally out of our control. It is simply the mating heat." When he looked down, he saw confusion in his mate's eyes. "Don't you know about the mating heat?"

Eli shook his head. "In case you didn't notice, my birth Pack is pretty repressed and conservative. It was forbidden to talk about sexuality and mating. Alpha

Steele said that such knowledge would come to a Shifter when it was necessary for them to have it." Eli's brows furrowed. "He kept us all ignorant, just so he could control us."

Kellan leaned down to place a gentle kiss on Eli's lips. "When mates first find each other, the attraction is there immediately. After their first intimate contact, they go into something akin to a 'mating heat'. Their need for each other becomes all-consuming and, for a few weeks, all they want to do is fuck like bunnies. It happens to every true mated pair and it is completely normal. After that first kiss at Sephora, it was only a matter of time until the mating heat brought us together." He squeezed Eli tighter. "I don't want you beating yourself up about this. Your brother is going to be fine and we are going to catch the asshole who hurt him. He might have thought your father was one scary SOB, but he hasn't met me yet. He'll be crying for his momma in minutes." Kellan flashed Eli an evil smile. Eli's return smile was small, but filled with a building hope.

Although he wished there was no need for it, Kellan was glad his mate allowed him to be there for him in his time of need. Eli was a powerful wolf in his own right. The fact that he was willing to let Kellan help him now worked to soothe the turmoil his wolf had been experiencing since the discovery of his mate. The need to protect his mate filled him and gave him new purpose. He would not allow anyone to hurt his mate or those dear to him. Carl Yager had made a fatal mistake and hadn't even realized it. Kellan was looking forward to showing him the error of his ways.

Chapter Eleven

A loud pounding on the door jerked them back to awareness. Kellan had to fight a smile when Eli's cheeks flamed, staining them an enticing pink that had Kellan licking his lips in anticipation. *Damn, his mate was gorgeous!* Craving a taste of his mate's amazing mouth, Kellan leaned in, only to find himself faced with Eli's disapproving scowl. Why did his mate have to pick now to be such a killjoy? Shooting one last glance at his mate, who was staring pointedly at the door, Kellan shrugged before going to see who was there.

Scenting the air as he approached, a smile spread across his face, unprompted. Flipping the lock and jerking open the door, he found Jai and Dylan waiting, not so patiently, in the hallway. Before he could so much as give a greeting, Kellan found himself being shoved out of the way by six plus feet of ornery Jaimeson Miller. Dylan trailed behind him, an amused expression on his face.

"My apologies, Alpha," his Beta said in his normal, stoic tone, eyes leveled on the floor at Kellan's feet.

"We did not mean to interrupt your time with your mate. We beg your forgiveness." When he took a knee, bowing his head and tilting it to the side in a sign of submission, Kellan had all he could do not to laugh. Dylan had always had a flair for the dramatic and tended to take himself far too seriously. Kellan had secretly hoped that Jai and Dylan would work out whatever issues there were between them and announce their mating to the Pack. Kellan could not imagine a more perfectly balanced pair...well, except for himself and Eli. With a little luck, Dylan would have a calming effect on the usually volatile, Jai, and Jai would encourage Dylan to lighten up and learn to have a little fun. Kellan was about to tell Dylan much the same thing, when Jai's irate voice filled the apartment.

"Oh, the hell we do!" he snarled, disgust and annoyance evident in his tone. "Dylan, get off your damn knees! This is my apartment and I have every right to come and go as I please. Besides, these assholes should be less concerned with their cocks and more concerned about what we're gonna do when Crazy Carl shows his face."

Kellan thought the whole rant was hilarious, until Jai turned a murderous glare at Eli. "I can understand Kellan doing something like this, everyone knows he only uses the little head for thinking, but Noah is your brother." Jai shook his head in disgust. "You guys need to get your shit together. Carl is a sociopath who enjoys inflicting pain on others. Have you even taken a minute to consider what he might have done to your brother, or were you too busy getting off to care?"

Jai turned to storm out of the room, but Kellan reached out a hand, grabbing him by the scruff of the neck. Kellan was willing to accept criticism from his friends and Pack mates, but he drew the line at anyone hassling his mate. The fact that Jai and Eli had been friends since childhood didn't matter to Kellan in the slightest. All it had taken was one look at Eli's face to see that Jai's angrily spewed words had hit a nerve with his mate. A look of shame and regret now marred the man's gorgeous face. Friend or no, Jai was going to learn that there were consequences that came with disrespecting the Alpha Mate.

Startled, Jai turned wide eyes on his Alpha, clearly unsure what was about to happen. Kellan was prepared to lay into his friend, when a throat cleared nearby. Looking over his shoulder, he found Dylan standing near his elbow, waiting to be addressed. Exasperated by the interruption, Kellan snarled at the man in response.

"Kellan," Dylan spoke out gently, obviously not wanting to further irritate his Alpha. "Please, allow me to handle this. He is my responsibility."

Surprised, Kellan quirked a brow in response to Dylan's declaration. He had never heard either man verbally recognize the importance of the other in their lives. The fact that Dylan had claimed responsibility for Jai spoke volumes as to what their relationship was, or should be.

Nodding his agreement, Kellan released his grip on Jai's neck, motioning for Dylan to take over, as he stepped to the side to watch the show. He saw apprehension fill Jai's eyes as Dylan took a step toward him, a stern expression clouding his face. When Jai went to take a step back, Dylan released a fierce growl, stopping him in his tracks.

"Easy, Dylan," Jai stammered. "What's your problem?"

"You will never speak that way to your Alpha again, pup!" Dylan snarled, forcing the words out through clenched teeth. With his eyes narrowed and nostrils flared, he looked every bit the warrior Kellan knew him to be. Gone was the gentle soul he preferred to present to the world. The man standing before them could easily rip an enemy to shreds without hesitation. As Dylan released another deep growl, Jai took a subtle step in Kellan's direction, as if hoping his Alpha would protect him from the big, bad Beta. Kellan smirked.

"So," Jai drawled nervously, "looks like you have a little spunk after all, Killer. Who knew?"

Kellan watched Dylan lean forward until his face was nearly buried in Jai's neck. He inhaled deeply and his eyes shuttered briefly, before he met Jai's incredulous gaze.

"While I normally enjoy your high-handed dominance, when it comes to the treatment of our Alpha and Alpha Mate, you will show them the proper respect, at all times. When it comes to the care and protection of the Alpha, I will always be in charge. However, I would gladly have you run the show in other arenas." Dylan's regard burned into him, both sizing him up and stripping him down, leaving no doubt as to what he had in mind.

Jai's mouth opened, then closed, like a fish out of water before he snapped it shut so hard the clink of his teeth was audible. A frown formed on his lips.

"When Hell freezes over," he sneered.

Dylan gave a subtle nod of his head as he took a step back, giving Kellan room to resume control of the conversation. "I can wait."

He turned fluidly and took a place of sentry next to the front door. He leaned against the wall with his arms folded across his chest, once again the calm, quiet, loyal man Kellan had known a good portion of his life. Once again, Kellan had to chuckle at the situation. If the two men ever got their acts together, their mating just might be one for the books…that is, if they didn't kill each other first.

Giving a bored yawn, Kellan glanced lazily between the two men. "If you guys are done with all your drama, I think we should let the others in so we can firm up our game plan. I think we've kept them waiting out there long enough." When neither man spoke against it, he opened the door and a flood of people surged in.

When Kellan saw his cousin, Dax, enter the room and head in his direction, he couldn't hide his smile. Large, barrel-chested and sporting miles upon miles of hard-packed muscle, the man was just plain massive. His arms were twice the size of a normal man's and his legs were like tree trunks. There were thick, silver rings through both ears, the hint of a tattoo peeking out of the collar of his shirt, and his honey-colored hair was spiked in artful disarray. Kellan was sure Eli had never met him before, judging by the look on his face, and Kellan couldn't wait to introduce them. As they were two of his favorite people in the world, he hoped that they would get along. Dax took a knee when he reached Kellan, tilting his head in acknowledgment.

"Alpha, the pack has been notified of the situation. We have wolves watching every road into town and more posted along the way here. There is no way he can enter our territory without being spotted. You will be notified as soon as he has been seen." His cousin remained on the floor, as if waiting for direction from his Alpha.

Kellan stepped forward, placing a large hand on the other man's shoulder. "Well done, Dax. Now, quit being a douchebag and get off your fucking knees! You know I hate that shit."

The large man glanced up, a shit-eating grin plastered on his face. "Alpha, whatever do you mean? I am only trying to show you the respect your position deserves."

Kellan smacked him on the back of the head before offering him a hand up. Dax was still chuckling at Kellan's disgruntled look. Kellan shook his head and wrapped a hand around Eli's arm, drawing him near.

"E, I'd like to introduce you to the biggest pain in the ass in the Pack, my cousin, Dax Marshall. Dax, this is my mate, Elijah Steele."

Dax looked Eli over like he was checking out his next meal. He even licked his lips, as if imagining what Eli would taste like. Kellan knew the man well enough to know that he would never try to poach his mate, but Kellan still did not like the interest he saw flare to life in his cousin's eyes. It was hard to stay mad, however, when the man in question graced him with a blinding smile, before turning his attention back to his mate.

"Well, hello, gorgeous! Mate, you say? Are you sure you want to stay with the ol' stick-in-the-mud here? The things I could do to that magnificent ass of yours..."

Without a thought, a menacing growl burst from Kellan's throat, interrupting whatever proposition his cousin had been about to make. Dax turned to meet his eyes and burst out laughing. It was a rich, happy sound that warmed Kellan to his toes, successfully melting away any irritation or anger he was feeling toward the other man. His humor was one of the things Kellan enjoyed the most about Dax, as well as being something that had a tendency to drive him out of his mind. Kellan sighed before giving the man a chagrined smile.

"As you can see, I am very fond of my mate. As it is still new and I appear to have become extremely possessive, I suggest you not mention trying to get in his ass for a while. My wolf doesn't seem to appreciate it."

Dax smiled fondly at Kellan. "Who would have ever thought you would be possessive of anyone? How does your ginger stalker feel about the new lay of the land?" He gave a subtle head nod toward the front door.

When Kellan followed his direction, he noticed Tracy leaning again the wall, his hate-filled eyes glaring maliciously at his mate. The look Eli sent back in return was something fearsome to behold. With his legs braced apart, jaw clenched and eyes gone cold, Eli appeared to be on the verge of attack. Kellan watched Tracy's scowl deepen before he moved away, disappearing into the gathered crowd.

That, of course, caused Dax's mirth to return threefold. The big man was laughing so hard, he was bent over at the waist, trying to catch his breath. When he finally regained some control over himself, he turned to Kellan's mate with a smile that could have lit the whole world.

"Eli, my man, you are a breath of fresh air! I've been telling Kellan for years to quit messing around with all those little boys that fawn all over him. He's always brushed me off when I told him that you haven't lived until you've had a big, muscled body riding your cock. Well, cousin," he said turning to Kellan, "do you now understand the difference between playing with a boy and scoring with a man?"

Kellan blushed, immediately embarrassed by the reminder of his past prejudice. Thankfully, he had learnt the error of his ways and he had never been more grateful for the lesson. There was no comparison between the quick encounters he'd had with men in the past and what he experienced when he was with his mate.

"Yes, Dax, I can, now, truly appreciate the difference you've tried to drill into my brain the last few years. Thank you. Your wisdom is immeasurable." He gave his cousin a mock bow before smacking him in the back of the head, yet again.

They were all still laughing when Dylan approached, his dark eyes serious, a grave expression shadowing his face. "I just got a call from Malachi. He was stationed one town over to the east and just saw a man matching Carl Yager's description driving a gray panel van. He's heading our way. Malachi estimates arrival in about thirty minutes." Just that quickly, playtime was over. The enemy was almost at their door.

Kellan surveyed the room with pride. When word had spread about the situation, he'd been flooded with calls from pack members volunteering their services. He'd actually had to start turning people away. It said a lot about the loyalty of his pack that so many would volunteer their help in this kind of situation. The men and women gathered around him signified the power of a healthy pack. He looked forward to Eli being able to experience it. The only thing that stood in the way was Alpha Charles Steele and his twisted machinations. The threat to his mate needed to be dealt with as quickly as possible. His first move in that effort was going to be dealing with Carl Yager.

Chapter Twelve

The planning of their course of action happened relatively quickly. That being the case, Eli was not totally convinced that their best plan should involve him sitting alone in the apartment, waiting for Carl Yager to show up. Eli had thought it best to try to intercept Carl on his way into town. That way they would be able to use their wolf forms, if necessary, without the added worry of being seen by the human population. Kellan had quickly vetoed that option, citing that it would be much easier to conceal all the assisting members of the pack throughout the neighboring apartments and the surrounding shops, than it would be to coordinate everyone in a large open expanse. He liked the idea of having a small, defensible area. Kellan's major concern was that Carl had lied to Eli and was not really alone. With an unknown number of enemy combatants en route, he felt it would be easier to protect Eli in the apartment building.

While Eli didn't necessarily agree that it was the best course of action, he knew arguing with Kellan in front of the pack would make Kellan look weak. He resigned himself to following along with the current plan and fighting with Kellan about his overbearingness at a later date, when there was more time to do it right.

Because Shifters had such a strong sense of smell, no one would be able to be in the apartment with Eli without running the risk of discovery. Therefore, Eli was alone in the living room, pacing. He would never forgive himself if he failed to get his brother back alive. All he could hope for was that Carl wasn't completely lost in his fantasy world and that he would still realize that the best way to get Eli to comply with his wishes would be to spare Noah's life.

After another twenty minutes of pacing a rut into the apartment floor, Eli finally heard the chime of the elevator down the hall. He tensed, knowing it had to be Carl. Part of the plan had been to evacuate the apartment building of all humans and redirect anyone other than Carl who attempted to enter. With the humans gone, pack members had been placed in the now vacant apartments throughout the building. Even if Carl picked up on the strong scent of shifters in the building, he would most likely assume it was a shifter owned building and therefore justify it to himself without suspicion.

A strong, double knock sounded through the apartment. Eli schooled his features, desperate to hide his apprehension from Carl. He knew he had a role to play if he had any hope of getting his brother back alive. There was no guarantee that Carl had brought Noah with him. He might have changed his mind, deciding to grab Eli and take his chances that Noah would survive the trip to Mason without medical attention. Reaching for the knob, Eli took a breath to calm his ragged nerves. Exhaling, he opened the door and was greeted with a sight straight out of his nightmares.

Carl Yager stood before him with Noah slung half over his shoulder. Eli's brother, on the other hand, looked like he had one foot in the grave and the other clinging to the edge. His face was a swollen mass of bruises and cuts. It looked like he had picked a fight with a meat grinder and come out the loser. As he was shirtless, Eli could see that his chest and arms were covered in a crisscross of deep, angry cuts. Some were so deep, Eli was sure he could see bone. His right wrist was swollen to twice its normal size and was hanging at an unnatural angle. As Eli's gaze wandered farther down Noah's body, he noticed that there were multiple slices through his jeans and blood was still seeping through most of them. Noah's shoes must have been taken at some point during his time with Carl because he was barefoot. His feet were bruised and, to Eli's horror, he was missing at least four toenails that Eli could see. The only thing that seemed to be going in Noah's favor was the fact that he wasn't conscious. The pain would have been excruciating.

Eli swallowed, trying to hold back the bile that was creeping up his throat. He had never wanted to kill anyone as much as he wanted to kill Carl Yager in that moment. The thought of what the psychopath had done to his brother was almost too much for Eli to bear.

He took a step toward Carl, determined to end his life in the most painful way possible. He was just within striking distance when he felt a warm, reassuring presence touch his mind. At first, Eli thought he had imagined it and tried to brush it off, all focus on his deadly intent. Another step toward Carl only made the feeling come back stronger. Eli was starting to feel like Carl's crazy might be catching when he heard Kellan's voice in his head.

"Eli, you need to calm down and stick to the plan."

"Kellan?" Eli's thoughts whispered back, in disbelief. *"What the hell?"*

"It's another aspect of the mating bond. We haven't had a chance to test it until now. You need to try to convince your wolf that killing Carl Yager is not in its best interest. We need to get information out of him and we can't interrogate a corpse." Kellan's tone was like a soothing balm on Eli's subconscious. Unfortunately, all it took was one look at Noah's bleeding, broken body, and his wolf's hackles were up and bloodlust was threatening to take over, once again.

"ELI! You have to stay calm! That is an order from your Alpha!"

Eli's snarl of fury echoed through his head. *"Kellan, you haven't seen what that fucker did to Noah! I'm not even sure if he's alive. Carl tortured him to within an inch of his life... He needs to die!"*

"Noah is not dead, Eli. I can sense it from here and you would be able to sense it, too, if you could just calm your wolf. At the moment, your wolf is only going to impede your judgment. You have to stay calm for just a little longer. Try to get some information from Carl and start treating Noah's injuries. I'll be with you the whole time. I love you."

Eli was momentarily stupefied by Kellan's proclamation. Kellan loved him? Well, he had chosen a really great time to let him in on that little secret. While Eli fumed, he swore he could hear Kellan's mental chuckle echoing through his head.

"You're an asshole, Kellan Reeves! I'm kicking your ass when this is over, so be prepared."

"Looking forward to it, babe."

Kellan's laughter filled his thoughts once again before he felt Kellan withdraw. Eli took a deep, calming breath before lifting his head to address the monster before him. Carl's face lit up in response to being the focus of Eli's attention. His face was filled with an odd, calculating pleasure, like a child debating the best way to rip the wings off a fly to keep it from flying away.

"Eli," Carl murmured.

Entering the apartment, Carl dropped Noah like a sack of potatoes, in his haste to get to Eli. He wrapped his beefy arms around Eli's waist, pulling him into a tight embrace. Carl buried his nose in Eli's neck and inhaled before moaning deeply in satisfaction. Eli took a moment to be grateful that Dax had suggested he shower and visit the building's steam room before Carl arrived so he wouldn't detect Kellan's scent on him. Never one to needlessly provoke a sleeping bear, Eli had followed his suggestion without question.

Satisfied that Carl had not picked up any scent of Kellan, Eli relaxed slightly. Carl seemed to interpret it as a sign of his acceptance and began placing butterfly kisses up and down Eli's neck. Eli's stomach rolled. His jaw clenched as he fought back the nausea and fury threatening to overcome him. He had to hold it together for a little while longer. They needed as much information as they could get from Carl about what Eli's father was planning. They could interrogate the man, but everyone was in agreement that his truthfulness would be less in doubt if Eli could ease the information out of him using this ruse.

"Fuck, Eli. You smell so good." Carl groaned into Eli's neck, rubbing his groin roughly against Eli's thigh. "Where's your bedroom?"

Carl's words brought a cold sweat to Eli's skin. No fucking way was he going to allow Carl to touch him like that. He had to do something to get this conversation moving in a direction he felt more comfortable with.

"Carl," Eli murmured, softly, "you don't want to risk angering my father by sleeping together before my official mating with the Tremmel girl, do you? He only agreed to let us be together after I mated her and got her pregnant." Eli placed a finger under Carl's chin, gently raising it to meet his eyes. "I don't think he will be pleased if he finds out we were together before he said he would allow it. If he got angry enough, he might not let us be together at all. You don't want to risk that, do you?"

Carl seemed to ponder his words, then let out a deep, resigned sigh. He thrust once more against Eli, before taking a step back. He ran a hand through his hair, making him look even more deranged.

"You're right, Eli," he groaned, roughly. "Of course, you're right. I've just wanted us to be together for so long, it's hard to fight my wolf's demand to mate. I can't tell you how hard it's been, all these years, knowing you were destined to be mine but not being able to touch you. Being forced to share a bed with that *woman*, when the only person I ever wanted to sleep with was you." Carl's eyes became unfocused. "Do you know that I used to sleep outside your bedroom window almost every night, to be close to you? I would watch you shower and get into bed naked, wishing I was in there with you. Every night, I jerked off to the image of your big, hard body dripping wet, bent over, ready to take me." He sighed again, momentarily lost in his dreamland visual.

Fighting back a shiver of revulsion, Eli turned his back on Carl, going to Noah's side to check his condition. Eli knelt next to his brother and rolled him over onto his back. He could make out the faint rise and fall of his chest, signaling that Noah had not yet lost the battle for life. Time, however, was not on his side. He needed immediate medical treatment if he was going to survive the night.

Rising to his feet, Eli went to the dining room table where he had stacked all the medical supplies the pack doctor had left for him. While he had only limited medical training, he knew enough to keep Noah alive until the pack doctor could take over for him. Quickly, he got to work cleaning and bandaging wounds while Carl watched him.

"Don't be upset, Eli. I only did what your father told me to do. He decided your brother needed to be taught a lesson. He told me Noah needed to remember who was Alpha and whose orders were meant to be followed. I know how much you care for him. I'm sure there is a possibility he can come back from this. I don't want this incident to come between us and keep you from enjoying all the things I'm going to do to you later."

"I believe you, Carl," Eli stated, trying to drum up as much false understanding as he could muster. It was hard, but his effort must have been enough because Carl seemed to relax. "I just don't understand why my father would make you do this. None of it makes any sense to me. Why hurt Noah? Why force us into marriages we don't want? Why not let you and I be together?" Eli sighed deeply, plastering a devastated look on his face. He even managed a few tears as he looked into Carl's eyes. "Why does this matter so much to him, Carl?" Eli pulled back, looking up at

Carl with bleary, tear-filled eyes. "Make me understand, Carl. Maybe if I knew why this was so important, it would be easier for me to accept and bear it, until we can finally be together."

"Of course, Eli. The last thing I want is for you to waste your energy worrying. You're going to need it later for more enjoyable activities." Carl ran a hand down Eli's back, following the path of his spine. Eli had all he could do to fight the urge to throw off his hand and break all of his fingers.

"Your father has been making plans to expand the pack territory," Carl continued, oblivious to Eli's disgust. "For the past few years, he has been infiltrating neighboring packs, searching for weaknesses, preparing to overthrow their Alphas and absorb the remaining pack members and land into our pack. If all goes according to plan, the Mason Pack will become the biggest, strongest pack in the United States. With that kind of power, no pack would dare to challenge us."

Eli's mouth dropped open and his eyes went wide. The idea of what his father was planning reaffirmed that the man was completely out of his mind. The Mason Pack was an average-sized pack having around fifty members. Nearly half of those, however, were women, children and elderly. How Charles Steele thought he would be able to take over a pack the size of Kellan's, whose numbers ran closer to five hundred members, was beyond Eli's ability to comprehend.

Eli nodded his head in feigned agreement. "All right, I get the concept of takeover and expansion but, honestly, how can he believe he will pull it off? The Mason Pack is small compared to some of the other packs in Michigan, let alone the rest of the country. How can he believe that this plan will work when there are packs in other states that number in the thousands?"

Carl smiled, conspiratorially. "That is where the marriage pacts come in. While scoping out rival packs in the surrounding areas, Alpha Steele managed to find many like-minded Shifters who wanted to join his cause. Mr Tremmel was among their number. Your father and his counsel of advisors know that in order for their plan to work, we have to plan for the future of our Pack. In a war, there are always casualties. By arranging strongly matched pairs, your father is setting our pack up to have a strong next generation of wolves. The children you will be breeding will bring our pack into the future and maintain its place at the top of Shifter society. These matches, helped along by a gift from Mr Tremmel's biochemical company, will breed the strongest Shifters in history."

Worry niggled in Eli's brain. "What special 'gift' is father getting from Mr Tremmel's company, Carl?"

Carl chuckled. "Mr Tremmel has had his scientists working on a chemical that can enhance strength, speed and intelligence in unborn fetuses. There are some hormones that both the mother and father are required to take before breeding is attempted. When conception is confirmed, an additional hormone is injected into the fetus. The results are amazing, E. These children will be like nothing the world has ever seen before."

Eli had to hand it to his father. When he decided to do something, he took it all the way. In this case, he took it all the way to Crazy Town, with a small pit stop in WTF! Eli was at a loss for what to say. However, Noah began seizing on the floor, ending the need for any further discussion on the matter.

Turning back to his brother's care, Eli saw that Noah was making a drastic turn for the worse. His skin had gone ashy, his lips were turning blue and the heartbeat Eli was trying to check for was almost non-existent.

"Kellan!" Eli's panicked shout sounded through their mental connection. *"There's no more time. I'm losing Noah! I need the doctor, NOW!"*

"On our way, E." Kellan's response was instantaneous, confirming Kellan's declaration that he would not leave him alone during the confrontation with Carl. Eli wasn't sure how much of his conversation with Carl Kellan had heard, but the look on his face when he entered the room, seconds later, let Eli know that whatever he'd heard would not mean good things for Carl.

Kellan's entire countenance was black. He entered the room as regal as a king with his eyes spitting fire, his jaw clenched tight and his gaze only for his mate. He went directly to Eli's side and pulled him into a bone-crushing embrace. Eli didn't even register the pain when, at the moment, all he needed was to feel whole again in Kellan's arms. He would never be able to un-hear the things Carl had told him, but with Kellan by his side, he knew he could put them behind him.

Chapter Thirteen

When they finally broke off their embrace, Kellan immediately started examining his mate for any possible injuries. Once he was convinced that his mate was still in good condition, he turned his attention back to the activity in the room. Two large Betas were forcing Carl to the floor, the pack doctor and an assistant were tending to Noah and another eight or more wolves were scattered throughout the living room, dining room and kitchen. With the immediate threat neutralized, Kellan felt a heavy weight lift off his chest as relief poured through him. Looking down at his mate, he saw the same relief echoed in Eli's eyes.

"You did great, babe." Kellan reached out a hand, brushing back Eli's hair before leaning down to place a kiss over his mating mark. "I wanted to kill him. When he touched you...when he said all those things to you... I wanted to rip him limb from limb. The only thing that stopped me was Dylan."

"Yeah." Jai smirked, throwing a glare over his shoulder at Carl, before making his way to Eli. "Dylan had to fight to keep him from running in here. They wrestled. It was incredibly hot." Jai threw a conspiratorial wink at Eli. "Don't worry, I got video of it on my phone. We can watch it later."

Kellan rolled his eyes at Jai before turning to stare at Carl who was now cuffed and sitting on one of the dining room chairs, flanked by the same large Betas that had taken him down. He didn't like the way Carl was staring at Eli, a look of cold calculation stamped on his face. Kellan growled at him, wrapping a large arm around Eli's waist and pulling him close.

"Mine!" Kellan roared, menace dripping from the word. "My mate!"

"No!" Carl snarled, his face morphing into a mask of fury. He leaned forward in his chair, as far as his bonds would allow. "Don't touch Eli. He was promised to me by his father. If you touch what is mine, I will butcher your pack, one by one. Every man, woman and child—bled out like pigs at slaughter. I will leave their mutilated corpses at your door, before I burn your city to the ground. Only then will I come for you..."

Kellan chuckled darkly. "Touch him? I own him—body, heart and soul, as he owns me in return. He is my destined mate. The idea that you thought to take what was fated to be mine makes me want to rip you apart, piece by piece. It's fortunate for you that you have information I need or your suffering would begin tonight."

Instead of cowering in fear as Kellan had expected, Carl's expression grew darker, near malevolent. "He is *my* mate! When the slaughter of your Pack begins, you will have only yourself to blame. I will never rest until I have him back. You will never be free of me."

Kellan sneered in contempt. "Malachi, Warden, get him secured and get one of the trucks ready for transport. I want him back at the Pack House and locked in a cell within the hour."

Giving his back to the prisoner, Kellan began handing out orders to the rest of the pack. The human residents needed to be allowed back into the building and given a plausible explanation for events. The doctor needed assistance getting Noah out of the building and back to the Pack House without being seen. The rest of the pack was on clean-up duty, divided between Carl's van and the route he'd taken through the apartment building, dragging Noah's blood-soaked body.

Within minutes, the apartment was practically a ghost town, leaving only Kellan, Eli, a few Betas and a very pissed off Carl, who was still tied to a chair. While logically Kellan knew Carl was restrained and wouldn't be able to get to Eli with him in the room, Kellan didn't like the idea of Carl even breathing the same air as his mate. He had just decided to have the prisoner moved into a different apartment, when his phone rang. A quick glance at the screen told him it was Malachi, and immediately, Kellan knew that whatever his Beta had to say wasn't going to make him happy. Pressing the button to connect the call, Kellan listened as Malachi passed along some rather upsetting news. Growling out additional orders, Kellan disconnected the call, snapping his phone closed with near shattering force. Out of the corner of his eye, he saw Eli cautiously approach. When the smaller man was within arm's reach, he grabbed his wrist and dragged him into the shelter of his arms. He took a minute to just breathe in the scent of his mate, anger and frustration warring inside him, desperate for a release.

"What's going on, Kel?" Eli asked, after a few minutes of silence.

Kellan sighed, knowing that no matter how much he'd prefer otherwise, he couldn't keep this from his mate. Kellan looked down, only to meet with Eli's concerned gaze. "The team I sent down to deal with Carl's van just called up to inform me that it's missing. They went to the location where we found it earlier, a few blocks away, and it's gone. It looks like the asshole was lying to you when he said he came here alone. Whoever was working with him took off with the van and is no doubt on their way back to report everything that's happened. So much for the element of surprise." He growled low in his throat, the sound filled with frustration and anger. "I was hoping to have some time to decide how we were going to handle this." He looked over, glaring at Carl. Carl's only reaction was to glare back, murderously.

"It just doesn't make sense," Eli muttered, thoughtfully.

"What doesn't make sense, E?"

Eli sighed. "I could have sworn that Carl was telling the truth when he told me that he was in town alone. I don't understand. Why would he lie about it? There was no reason for him to keep it a secret. He already had all the leverage he needed to get me to agree with his demands, just by having Noah. It just doesn't make sense."

"The man is out of his mind, Eli. It would be a miracle if any of the things that came out of his mouth were true. He is obsessed with you and he will say anything to try to make you his. You can't trust anything he says," Kellan growled.

Eli shrugged. "If you're sure..."

Kellan gave him a smile. "I'm sure. Now, I want to move Carl into one of the empty apartments down the hall while we're waiting for Malachi and Warden to get back with the truck for transport. I think my wolf and I will both feel more at ease if Carl isn't near you anymore. I'm still feeling pretty edgy."

Edgy might be putting it lightly. Ever since Carl had entered the building dragging a bloody and broken Noah behind him, Kellan had felt that something was wrong. He'd assumed that once they had Carl in custody, the feeling would dissipate. Unfortunately, that couldn't have been further from the truth. Despite how things looked, Kellan knew that something wasn't right. Sadly, he had no way of knowing what the problem was.

Calling over the remaining Betas still in the apartment, they worked together to relocate Carl, chair and all, out of the apartment and down the hall, as far away as they could get him, while still being on the same floor. Kellan had to admit, just by having the additional separation between Carl and his mate, he was already feeling some of his nervous energy burn away.

Leaving his Betas temporarily in charge of guarding the prisoner, Kellan returned to Jai's apartment to check on his mate. He found Eli in the living room, cleaning up the evidence of the tussle between Carl and Kellan's Betas when they'd struggled to apprehend him.

Closing the distance between them, Kellan pulled Eli into his arms, holding him tight against his heart. "I have to head back down the hall to help keep an eye on Carl, until Malachi and Warden get back. Are you going to be all right?"

Eli smiled, reassuringly. "I'll be fine. I was thinking about taking a quick shower, if you think that would be okay."

"I would appreciate that," Kellan said, softly, brushing a light kiss to the back of Eli's neck. "The smell of another man on you is driving my wolf crazy."

"Just your wolf?"

Kellan's eyes darkened, giving Eli his answer. Kellan hesitated for a moment, not quite sure how to pose the question he really wanted to ask. "You could pack a few changes of clothes to have at the house...you know...if you wanted to keep some there, for emergencies."

Eli wrapped his arms more firmly around Kellan's waist. "I suppose I could pack a few changes of clothes to keep at the Pack House. It kinda seems like a waste of time, though, when I'm just going to be packing up the rest of my stuff and bringing it over there in the next few days anyway."

It only took Kellan a minute to process what Eli had said. When he finally wrapped his mind around it, he almost shouted in triumph. "You're sure about this, E? Don't get me wrong, I definitely want you there — in my house, in my bed, in my life. I just don't want to pressure you. I'm willing to wait as long as it takes."

Kellan hated the words he was forced to say. Unfortunately, he knew he had to give Eli the chance to back away from this decision if he wasn't ready. As Alpha, he knew he wouldn't be able to forgive himself if he thought he had coerced Eli into accepting his position as Alpha Mate. He braced himself for the possible rejection, as he waited for Eli's response. He wasn't prepared for the laughter that seemed to explode from his mate.

"Christ, Kellan! You sure think a lot of yourself, don't ya?" Eli looked like he was on the verge of rolling on the floor in his mirth. "Do you honestly think you could force me to do anything I didn't want to do? You must really think you're hot shit, huh?"

Kellan scowled as his mate continued to laugh uncontrollably. When Eli finally gained control of himself, Kellan gently took his face between his large hands. "I love you, Eli. You are my mate and there is nothing I wouldn't do for you or give you. I just don't want you to feel like you have to accept this because I say it's right. It's not a decision you have to make today. Take all the time you need because once you agree to be mine, there will be no going back. When you and your wolf accept me, there will never be another for either of us... And to answer your other question...of course I think I'm hot shit."

That statement seemed to change something in Eli. Kellan watched as his mate's eyes went wide and his chest started to rise and fall rapidly. His eyes went soft and wet, then suddenly, Kellan had an armful of sexy and amazing Eli Steele. The fierceness of his embrace told Kellan everything Eli couldn't put into words — Eli loved him.

The swell of emotion building within him was nearly overwhelming. Twining his fingers in the hair at Eli's nape, he pulled his head back, forcing Eli to meet his gaze. "I love you, too, E. Does this mean you've made your decision?" Kellan's raised brow emphasized the questions.

The smile Eli graced him with could have lit the whole world with its brilliance. Eli grabbed Kellan's face with both hands, ravaging his mouth with a bruising kiss. They fed from each other, tongues twining, teeth nipping. Lost in their mutual passion, they didn't break from their joining until Eli's back slammed into the wall, shocking both of them from their revelry. Eli shrugged at Kellan sheepishly while Kellan merely laughed, pulling him into the warmth and comfort of his arms. He gave Eli one last soul-searing kiss before stepping away.

"Go. Get showered and packed. It should only take about ten minutes for Malachi and Warden to get here with the transport and restraints, so hurry. However, when we get back to the Pack House, we will be continuing this…conversation."

"Looking forward to it." Eli smirked.

Kellan smiled at his mate's play on his own, earlier words. The grin he gave Eli was wicked, bringing a flush to his mate's cheeks. Laughing, Eli blew him a kiss and headed in the direction of the bathroom. Kellan managed to pop him a good one on the butt before Eli rushed from the room. The sound of the shower running reached his ears a moment later and Kellan knew he needed to get moving. He wanted to get this over with so he could spend the rest of his evening exploring his mate's naked body, in bed.

He made his way out of the door, closing it securely behind him, before heading back down the hall to where Carl was being held. Kellan couldn't wait for this part of the day to be over with. All he wanted was to get back to his mate as fast as possible.

Re-entering the apartment, Kellan was shocked to see that Tracy and some of his friends from the club had arrived in his absence. The two Betas he had left in charge of guarding the prisoner, Mark and Eric, were now lounging in the living room while the smaller men fawned and preened all over them. Tracy was currently draped across Eric's lap, grinding his ass against the man's groin, while the big Beta rutted up against him. Carl, still tied to his chair, was watching the scene from his corner, a look of curious amusement on his face.

Kellan expected to feel some residual hurt or jealousy at finding his ex-lover in such a compromising position. However, after giving himself a moment to take in the scene, all he felt was disgust and annoyance. Finding Eli, his destined mate, truly had rid him of any attraction or desire he may have felt for any of his past lovers. Eli was all he could see, and he couldn't be happier about it. His wait was finally over.

Walking farther into the room, still unnoticed, Kellan looked on in irritation for another minute or two, before clearing his throat loudly. Five heads jerked in his direction. "What the hell is going on in here?" he growled, glaring at his Betas. Both men shot out of their seats, guilt clear in their expressions. Eric's quick rise caused Tracy to fall to the floor in a very undignified heap. Kellan would have laughed, if it wouldn't have detracted from the seriousness of the situation. The bigger of the two Betas, Marc, stepped forward, eyes firmly on the ground, head tilted in submission.

"A...Alpha, please, let me explain? Tracy was looking for you, so I told him he could wait here for you to return. Unfortunately, Tracy and his friends decided to have a bit of fun while they waited and, as you can see, Erik and I got a little distracted. Our apologies, Alpha."

While Kellan was far from pleased with the men's behavior, he knew from past experience that they were both loyal and hard-working. They reported directly to Dylan and Kellan knew there was no way Dylan would risk his safety, or the safety of his mate, by placing them with guards that couldn't be trusted. No, there was no doubt in his mind who was to blame for the lapse in security.

Growling his displeasure at the big men one last time, Kellan turned his attention to Tracy, who had managed to pull himself off the ground and was walking toward him, hips swaying saucily. He had to admit, his ex-lover looked amazing. Kellan would have assumed he was on his way out to a club, rather than volunteering to help catch a fugitive. With his skin-tight clothes and glossy lips, he looked like he was on the prowl.

"What are you doing here, Tracy?" Kellan asked, suspiciously.

Tracy stuck out his full bottom lip in a pout. "Is there something wrong with a guy wanting to be there for his man, in a dangerous situation?"

"Your man?" Kellan asked, cocking a brow. "And who would that be?"

Tracy threw his head back and laughed. "Well, you of course," he purred. "There is no way I could have just sat at home while you were out here trying to catch that terrible man. What if you'd been hurt? I'd never forgive myself." Tracy gave an exaggerated shudder that made Kellan want to roll his eyes.

How had he never realized how fake the other man was? The kind, caring man he had thought he'd been involved with didn't exist within this vapid, self-centered creature. While Kellan had always known he was not Tracy's only lover, he had believed their relationship had been based on mutual affection and respect. With his blinders removed, he could clearly see that the only thing that had driven their relationship was Tracy's desire for power and status. As Alpha Mate, he would have had both, in abundance. Kellan gave a very real shudder, thinking of how close he had been to giving up his search for his true mate, and accepting Tracy as his next best alternative. Eli's arrival couldn't have come at a better time.

Tracy moved forward, pressing himself tight to Kellan's body, undulating against him like some boneless reptile. Pressing his hands against Kellan's chest, he lowered them slowly, making a path south with one obvious direction in mind. Kellan couldn't believe his audacity. He allowed Tracy a little leeway, wanting to see how far he would take this pathetic excuse for seduction. His small hands had just reached Kellan's belt, with no signs of stopping, when Kellan couldn't stand another second of his touch.

Grabbing Tracy's wrists in a firm grip, Kellan forcibly removed his questing hands from his body. Tracy looked up at him, confusion clear on his face. Kellan snarled in response. "If what I just walked in on is your idea of being here to support me, I think I'll pass. I thank the gods for bringing Eli into my life when they did, and keeping me from nearly making the biggest mistake of my life."

Tracy's eyes burned with anger. Despite his best efforts, he was unable to hold onto his expression of hurt and confusion. "I don't understand how Eli has anything to do with our relationship. As for what you walked in on, you know I've always been a free spirit. Once we are officially mated, you know I'll only be with you. This doesn't change our relationship, or the way I feel about you." Tracy's eyes became soft and wet, brimming with feigned tears. "I have waited, all these years, for you to finally see what has been right in front of you—we are mates, Kellan. I am destined to be yours." Tracy leaned toward him, eyes wide and pleading.

"Mine?" Kellan's words were filled with mockery. "Even if you ignore the lack of mating heat, you've never been mine, Tracy. You give yourself to anyone, and everyone, and that is fine with me. I understood, and approved of, the parameters of our *relationship*. The fact that you've confused the mediocre sex we shared with a mating, destined by the gods, is sad and, quite frankly, insulting. The idea that I would be gifted with such a conniving and faithless mate truly speaks to how little you think of me," Kellan snarled. "Thankfully, the gods must not share your low opinion. Elijah Steele is my true mate. A fact that has made me eternally grateful."

The look of shock on Tracy's face brought him a moment of satisfaction. When the man remained speechless, Kellan turned his attention back to his Betas. "I need some air. I'm going to run down and check on everyone's progress. I'll be back within ten minutes. When I return, I expect to find only the two of you, and your prisoner here. Understood?" Kellan glared at the men, leaving no doubt about his demands.

"Yes, Alpha!" the men replied instantly. Kellan's respect for the men went up, slightly, at their quick response. Maybe there was hope for them yet. Heading for the door, Kellan pointedly ignored the angry expression on Tracy's face. As far as he was concerned, the only place the other man had in his life was in his past. Eli was his future, and Kellan couldn't wait to get their current mess behind them so they could start enjoying it.

Chapter Fourteen

Eli stepped out of the shower and briskly dried off his body with a towel from the nearby rack. He heard movement in the living room, signaling Kellan's return with Malachi and Warden. Eli went to his room to dress and quickly pack up a few changes of clothing. They would have to tide him over until he could pack up the rest of his things and have them moved over to the Pack House. He had no reservations about his decision. He knew that the only place he wanted to be was with Kellan, whose personal residence took up the entire top floor of the five-story Pack House. With Eli's acceptance of their mating came the knowledge that he never wanted to spend another night away from his mate. Moving into the Pack House was the next logical step.

Grabbing his duffel bag off the end of the bed, Eli made his way to the front of the apartment. He was just about to call out to Kellan when he noticed a familiar scent. His wolf's hackles immediately rose and a growl rumbled from his chest. *What the hell is he doing here?*

Eli entered the living room, ready to kick some ass. He wasn't prepared, however, to find Carl Yager reclining carelessly on the couch, unrestrained. Eli's blood ran cold at the implications of what had happened. Carl's eyes never left his face as he slowly tried to take a step back out of the room. Unfortunately, his progress was interrupted when he ran into something warm and solid. A quick look over his shoulder confirmed what Eli had sensed, only moments earlier. Standing directly behind him, arms crossed, scowling darkly, was Kellan's ex, Tracy.

"What have you done, Tracy?" Eli attempted to keep his voice calm as he tried to reason out what was happening.

Tracy smiled maliciously. "Nothing, really. Some friends from the club and I just went and paid a little visit to Mark and Eric, the guys Kellan left in charge of keeping an eye on Carl, here." Tracy laughed. "Big, dumb Betas never saw it coming. When they look at us, all they see are poor, defenseless *twinks* that need some big, strong man to take care of them. They were out cold, drooling on the carpet, before they even knew what happened. Maybe next time, they'll be more careful who they invite in for a visit." Tracy's tone was dripping with hate and revulsion. He turned, fixing a glare on Eli that would have taken him out on the spot, if looks could kill. "You thought you could just walk into this pack, take Kellan from me, and I would let you get away with it? Not going to happen! Kellan was going to be *my* mate. He was so close to giving up the idea of 'destined mates'. He was tired of waiting, and I just knew he was going to ask me to be his chosen mate. Then you had to waltz into town, throwing around your superiority and your Beta pheromones and he didn't stand a chance. What I don't get is why you even want him when you're not gay?"

"Look who's talking! I felt sorry for you when we found out that Kellan and I were mates. Everyone told me not to bother because you were just fuck buddies and that when Kellan wasn't around, you were out, spreading your ass for anything willing to stick it to ya. How does that translate to Kellan being your fated mate?"

Tracy ignored Eli's jab, continuing on with his tirade undeterred. With his rage riding him, he probably hadn't heard a word Eli had said. "It's because you want to be Alpha, isn't it?" Tracy's eyes were crazed, as he threw wild accusations at Eli. "You figured you could mate Kellan and then once it was official, you would kill him and take over the pack. You don't have to admit it, because I know I'm right. Well, I'm not going to let you take what's rightfully mine!" Tracy sneered at him. "When I saw how infatuated Kellan was with you earlier, I knew I had to do something before you were able to destroy him, and this Pack.

Originally I was just planning to kill you, but when Carl came into the picture, things just got so much more interesting. Killing you, while definitely satisfying, wouldn't subject you to the kind of suffering I feel you deserve for coming between Kellan and I. However, after hearing about your reaction to Carl's affections, I figured a trip back home was just what the doctor ordered. Carl and I had a little chat after we took care of the guards and came to an agreement. I promised I wouldn't kill you, and Carl promised he would take you back to your old pack and never let you set foot here again. He promised that once he mated you, he would break you, teach you to submit, and you would spend the rest of your days doing exactly what he said." Tracy smiled, maniacally. "I find I enjoy the idea of someone breaking you and turning you into their bitch! Maybe I'll have him send me pictures. I'd love to see you crawl on your hands and knees, begging. I think it's going to be my new fantasy."

Laughing to himself, Tracy threw a set of car keys to Carl, who had since risen from the couch. "You need to get out of here," Tracy advised. "Kellan should be back up here any minute. If they catch the two of us here, they won't bother to interrogate you. They will kill us both, on the spot."

Eli knew he was in trouble. He was hoping he could stall long enough to give Kellan time to make it back upstairs and recapture Carl before he had a chance to escape and warn Eli's father that the Grand Rapids Pack was on to his plan. Eli knew he had been right to believe Carl when he said he had come alone to retrieve Noah and Eli. It seemed Carl had found all the help he would ever need right in Kellan's own pack. When Kellan found out, he would be devastated.

Slowly, Eli started backing away down the hall, hoping Carl and Tracy would be too busy planning their escape to notice him slipping away. He had just reached his bedroom doorway when a strong hand grabbed his shoulder and spun him around, bringing him face to face with Carl Yager.

"Eli," he murmured sternly. "Where do you think you're going?"

"I was just..." Eli stammered, grasping for something plausible Carl might believe.

"Hush, now." Carl shook his head disappointedly at Eli. "I know that evil man brainwashed you into believing that you're his mate. Once I get you home, we're gonna have all the time in the world to fix what he's done and show you that you and I were meant to be together."

The smile that formed on his face made Eli's stomach churn. He could imagine what Carl had in mind for convincing him. He only hoped that Kellan would get there before Carl had time to attempt anything.

"Carl..." Eli began, trying to figure out a way to talk some sense into the crazy man. A flicker of something sane flashed in Carl's eyes, causing Eli to think he might have a chance, right before he felt a prick in his neck. Turning, he saw Tracy standing next to him with an empty syringe in his hand and an unsettling grin on his face.

"Sometimes it's the smallest things that can do the most damage. Now, now, Eli," he said condescendingly. "Let's just get you back home and away from Kellan's evil intentions. Don't worry about a thing. I'll make sure he understands that you aren't interested in seeing him anymore and you just focus on your new life with Carl and the Mason Pack, okay? I'll make sure Kellan is well taken care of."

The mockery in his tone made Eli want to punch him in the face, but his body was growing heavier and heavier. His head lolled forward, setting him off balance and sending him crashing to the floor. When he attempted to sit up, he found his limbs were too heavy to move.

"You'll never...get...away with this..." Eli gasped. He struggled to form words as his throat began to feel swollen and thick. Whatever Tracy had injected him with was working fast. "Your...scent... Kellan will...recognize..."

Tracy laughed, dismissing Eli's concerns with a wave of his hand. "Kellan will disregard any trace of my scent as being left behind when I was in the apartment earlier. He'll have no reason to suspect me, especially after I leave him a different trail to follow." Reaching into a bag by the door, Tracy smirked as he pulled out a wad of dirty laundry. "An old bed buddy left some clothes behind after we ended our relationship. I never would have guessed they'd be so useful to me." Eli was able to pick up the scent of an unfamiliar human, as Tracy hurried around the apartment, rubbing the soiled material across random surfaces in an effort to transfer the scent of the stranger, leaving behind a false trail for Kellan to find.

Eli managed a low noise of protest, but quickly realized he wasn't able to do much else. Tracy's mystery drug seemed to have fully kicked in, draining him of energy and rendering him unable to move or speak. Thankfully, the rest of his senses seemed to remain unaffected. With everything else going to hell, at least he had one thing in his favor. Eli closed his eyes and slowed his breathing, praying his performance would be enough to fool his captors.

It seemed to work, as the two men left him lying on the living room floor while they made their way into the kitchen, talking in hushed voices. Eli strained his ears, trying to make out what they were saying. He was able to piece together enough of the conversation to deduce that they were trying to plan Carl and Eli's exit from the building. With their limited time, it didn't take them long to make a decision.

It was simple. Tracy would create a distraction and act as lookout. Meanwhile, Carl would carry the 'unconscious' Eli down the back stairway and to his van. It turned out that one of Tracy's 'minions' from the club had been the one to move Carl's van. He had spotted it earlier and hidden it a few blocks away. They'd been hoping to cause enough chaos that Tracy could sneak into Jai's apartment and kill Eli, with no one being the wiser. Eli knew he was running out of time. If only he knew more about the mate bond he had with Kellan, maybe he could send him a message letting him know what was going on. Unfortunately, Eli wasn't sure how Kellan had sent him his thoughts earlier and no idea how to attempt the act himself. No matter how many times he tried, he got no indication from Kellan that the message was getting through.

The sound of approaching footsteps had Eli, once again, slowing his breathing in hopes his ruse would continue to be successful. He tried to remain motionless as one set of feet came to a stop mere inches from him. He heard shoes shuffling on the hardwood and deep breathing next to his ear. Eli wasn't sure which one of the crazies it was and wasn't sure which one he should be hoping for. He didn't have long to wonder.

"I just wanted to take a moment to say goodbye." Tracy's voice was soft and would have been soothing if he wasn't a complete nutcase who was giving Eli to an obsessed stalker like a gift-wrapped present. "You know, if you hadn't been trying to steal my soulmate, we could have been friends. I'm going to take such good care of Kellan, he's going to forget about you in no time. I still can't believe you almost convinced him that the two of you were mates, I mean, really? You're barely even gay. Kellan can do so much better... In fact, he's going to do better. He's going to do me!"

Tracy giggled like a teenage girl and Eli had all he could do to fight the urge to hurl. He felt a brief press of lips against his forehead, then Tracy was gone. Eli heard him cross the room and exit the apartment.

The knowledge that he was now alone with Carl had Eli breaking out in a cold sweat. He had no idea where Carl was and the fact that Eli was completely helpless was terrifying. His wolf was not handling their current situation well, either, and was starting to freak out. Eli could feel it pacing and snarling within him. If only he could shift, maybe his wolf would be able to fight the effects of the drug he'd been injected with. Unfortunately, his wolf was so agitated by the situation, there was no way he could focus enough to even attempt the change.

Accepting the fact that, for the time being, he was physically helpless, Eli focused all his energy on sending a warning to Kellan. Again, he felt nothing. In a last ditch effort, he tapped into his wolf, having it attempt to communicate with Kellan's wolf. When he was greeted with more silence, Eli was convinced he had failed, yet again. Just as he was accepting his failure, he heard a soft whine in his head. At first, he believed it was his own wolf and ignored it. The whine, however, became louder and more insistent. When he still refused to acknowledge the wolf, it became a forceful growl Eli would have recognized anywhere—it was Kellan's wolf. Eli wasn't sure how to go about communicating with the wolf but did his best with the time he had.

He was still trying to convey a message to Kellan's wolf when he heard Carl re-enter the living room. His steps were sure as he made his way over to Eli. He crouched for a moment before hoisting Eli's limp body over his shoulder and exiting the apartment. Quietly, he made his way down the hall, to the back stairwell. Eli listened, desperately hoping to hear a member of the pack coming to rescue him. Of course, his luck could not be that good. Carl made it to the first floor and out of the back entrance of the apartment building without running into any pack members or residents of the building. He broke into a jog as he cleared the rear parking lot. Eli was jostled so hard against Carl's shoulder, he was sure he was seconds from throwing up all over him. Eli couldn't think of anyone who deserved it more, except maybe Tracy.

He wasn't sure whether he should be more relieved or more worried when Carl slowed his jog down to a mere trot. As he rounded the corner of a park, Eli saw the van parked at a meter. Shifting his grip on Eli, Carl pulled the keys from his pocket and opened the sliding back door. Gently, he laid Eli on the floor in the back of the van. Eli felt a large hand brush his cheek, while the other ran fingers through his hair. He wanted to shrink away from the touch but knew to do so would give away the only advantage he had left.

The door closed moments later, leaving him in complete darkness. He felt the van shudder, as the engine roared to life. Knowing the chances of being found alive would drop drastically if he was taken to a new location, he desperately tried to reach Kellan through their bond. For a moment, he could have sworn he felt Kellan in his mind, but it was gone just as fast as it appeared. When the lurching of the van signaled its departure, Eli's worst fears were realized. His only hope was that his pleas to Kellan had been heard.

Chapter Fifteen

Kellan was on his way back up to the apartment when he was struck by the strangest sensation. For a moment, he could have sworn he had heard Eli calling out to him. It was small, like the tail end of an echo in the back of his mind. There one minute, gone the next. He was sure he must have imagined it.

Unsettled, Kellan reached out, attempting to touch his mate's thoughts, needing the reassurance that all was well. Focusing on his mate, he felt for their connection and was stunned when he came up empty. He still had a faint sense of their bond, but there was a disruption, like static over a phone line. No matter how hard he tried, there was still a wall, negating his efforts to reach his mate.

Fear, the likes of which he had never known, clawed at his insides. Racing up the stairs, he was at the apartment door in seconds, kicking it in and storming inside in a panic. A hurried inspection turned up nothing out of the ordinary. Nothing seemed out of place and there weren't any signs of a struggle. If Kellan hadn't known better, he would have assumed

Eli was out at the grocery store, or somewhere else equally mundane. Quickly placed calls to Jai, Dylan, Malachi and even Eli's own phone didn't turn up anything new.

Throwing himself down onto the couch, Kellan glared at the ceiling as he ran through all the possible scenarios of what could have happened to his missing mate. Taking in a deep breath, Kellan scented the room. Not expecting to find much, he worked to sort through and separate each individual scent profile. To Kellan's surprise, he immediately encountered an unfamiliar scent. Hope grew within him. Working his way through the apartment, room by room, Kellan looked for even the most minute trace of the stranger's scent.

As he began his search, he realized right away that something wasn't right. While the scent was spread out and easy to locate throughout the apartment, it was all superficial. Even if someone had managed to get the drop on Eli and incapacitate him without a fight, his abductor would still have had to pick him up and carry him from the apartment. His mate was a good-sized man. There would be no way to move him without bumping into a piece of furniture or brushing against the wall, in which case the scent would be much stronger, richer. In that moment, Kellan realized that he had been played. The scent that had given him new hope was just an elaborate ruse to lead him away from Eli's true abductor. With that knowledge, Kellan was convinced that whoever was responsible for Eli's disappearance had been in the apartment earlier in the day, causing their scent to blend in with the crowd.

Immediately, Kellan renewed his efforts. He was nearing the back of the apartment when he found it. The scent was faint, but still lingering in the air, like a blinking neon sign, demanding attention. Cherries, cinnamon and something sugary sweet. Tracy. *What the hell was he doing this far into Jai's apartment?* Kellan knew for a fact that Jai couldn't stand the man, and that was before Kellan had told him that Eli was his mate. He couldn't imagine his friend feeling any more charitable toward the smaller man now, especially since Tracy had done nothing to hide the fact that he still imagined himself to be Kellan's mate.

Kellan searched the rest of the apartment for the scent but was able to determine that his ex hadn't gone any farther into the apartment than the door to Eli's bedroom. While there was nothing definitive that pointed out Tracy's involvement, Kellan had learnt a long time ago to trust his instincts and right now, they were practically screaming out to him that his ex-lover had had something to do with his mate's disappearance. With no other clues to his mate's whereabouts, Kellan knew his best bet was to find Tracy and try to get some answers from him. He would do anything necessary to get the information out of the smaller man. Kellan recognized at that moment that past friendships meant nothing in the face of losing his mate. He would go through anyone, friend or foe, who stood between them.

Following Tracy's scent back through the apartment, something tugged at the back of his thoughts. As the thought became clearer, Kellan found himself once again filled with fear for his mate. He knew he needed to follow the scent back to its source. Acting on instinct, he found himself leaving the apartment and making his way down the hall. The farther he went, the clearer and more real his suspicions became. When he reached the door at the opposite end of the floor,

Kellan's stomach filled with dread, knowing what he would find when he entered the apartment.

Trying the knob, he was met with no resistance. Pushing open the door, his suspicions became reality. He found his Betas, Mark and Eric, sprawled on the floor, unconscious but, thankfully, alive. Tracy and his crew had cleared out and from the looks of it they had decided to perform their own version of a freedom run. Kellan entered the living room and looked to the far corner where Carl had previously been restrained. While his chair was still in the same spot, the seat was now empty. The ropes, cuffs and other various restraints were now lying neatly piled on a coffee table, nearby.

A wave of rage crashed into him at the confirmation of what had happened. He drove his fist into the wall, the force behind the hit breaking through drywall, wood and insulation, before coming clear out the other side. His hand throbbed as the haze of anger started to dull, allowing him to focus his thoughts. Turning his back on his act of destruction, Kellan pulled his phone from his pocket and placed a call.

Thankfully, Dylan knew to be waiting on his call and answered on the first ring. "Alpha?" His Beta's cool, calm voice washed over him, further soothing his rage and settling his nerves.

"Tracy is working with Carl Yager. He released him and, from the looks of things, helped him abduct my mate. All three of them are missing, and Mark and Eric are alive, but unconscious. I think they may have been drugged, which could also explain why I haven't been able to reach Eli through our mate bond."

"What's our next move?" Kellan was grateful for Dylan's single-minded focus. It helped keep him grounded and focused on what needed to be done.

"I want teams spread throughout the area looking for Carl, his van and Eli. If he's managed to get free of Carl, he may be out there, on foot and stranded. They can't have been gone more than ten minutes so I want them to start at a five mile radius and work their way out, in zones. Hopefully, that will minimize their chances of making it out of the area. Under no circumstances do I want him making it back to Mason with my mate. Is that understood?"

"Yes, Alpha." Dylan's response was immediate.

"I also want a team assigned to apprehend Tracy and his friends. They were involved in this. How involved, I'm not sure, but until I am, treat them as guilty until proven innocent. I'm not willing to take the chance of one of them calling to warn Carl that we are on to him. I need them all found and questioned as soon as possible. Hopefully, at least one of them may have an idea where he is taking my mate. I'm hoping we'll get lucky and he may be holed up somewhere, waiting for us to relax our search."

"I'm on it, sir," Dylan answered, confidently. "We'll find him, Alpha."

"Thank you, Dylan. I appreciate that."

"Where do you want Tracy and his conspirators brought for questioning, when they've been found?"

Kellan growled, thinking of what he would truly like to do to any of the men who may have helped deliver his mate into the hands of a madman. "I want them in separate holding cells at the Pack House. Until I say otherwise, they are to be treated as prisoners of war."

"Yes, sir. Do you want me to head out with one of the teams searching for Eli or do you want me tracking Tracy?"

"Bring Jai, and meet me back at the Pack House. We will head out together and start looking for Eli. He is the only thing that matters. Let the others worry about Tracy and his pack of vultures. There will be time to deal with them later, once my mate is back home, where he belongs." Kellan snarled, menacingly. "Let's hope, for their sakes, that he is returned, unharmed."

"Yes, Alpha," Dylan agreed, solemnly.

Chapter Sixteen

A sudden pitch of the van jerked Eli from his fitful dozing. He had no idea how long they had been traveling, but after what had to have been hours, he'd allowed himself to sleep, hoping it might help burn through the drug that was still rendering his body useless. Cautiously, he tested himself, hoping for any sign of improvement. Finally on the receiving end of some good luck, he found he had regained control of most of his body. His limbs still felt heavy and sluggish, but at least he could move again. He flexed his fingers and toes, trying to encourage blood flow into his stiff muscles.

The van stopped, bringing his attention back to his current situation. The driver's door squeaked open, then slammed shut, informing him that his captor was no longer inside it. While he desperately wanted to locate him, he didn't want to give away the improvement in his condition. Pulling on his wolf's senses, he focused on the sounds and scents around him. He found Carl quickly. The man sounded to be a few feet away from the van and was carrying on a heated conversation. Eli assumed it was over the phone since he couldn't make out the other side of the conversation, but he wasn't completely discounting the possibility that Carl was talking to the voices in his head. The guy was completely fucking nuts.

The conversation lasted a few more minutes before he heard Carl let loose a loud stream of expletives. *I guess that conversation didn't go well*, Eli thought to himself. Hearing approaching footsteps, Eli once again feigned sleep, hoping the act would continue to work a bit longer, while he planned his next move.

The side door rolled open and Carl's scent reached him, causing bile to rise in his throat. Eli had officially had enough quality time with Carl. He heard the man climb in the van and crawl over next to his prone form. He felt Carl's breath on his face and a large hand cup his cheek. The seconds ticking by felt like an eternity and Eli wasn't sure how much longer he could keep his shit together. His wolf was riding him hard to rip out the throat of the man who had caused them to be separated from their mate. Needless to say, it was not in a forgiving mood.

Carl sighed, deeply. "I'm gonna run into the gas station real quick, baby, and get something for you to eat and drink when you wake up. I'm getting a little worried about ya, here. That prissy little pretty boy swore that shit he gave ya would only put ya out for an hour or two. I might have to pay the little bitch boy a visit for lyin' to me. He better not have hurt ya or I'll have to take that out of his hide, too. Something was not right with that guy. Messed up in the head, for sure."

Eli wanted to laugh at the ridiculousness of Carl calling anyone messed up in the head. Talk about the pot and the kettle. Eli felt dry lips press against his cheek, then Carl was pulling away. The van dipped and the door slammed shut, leaving Eli blessedly alone. He waited another minute for Carl to move beyond hearing distance before he forced himself to sit up. It was hard as hell but doable. All of his muscles were tight and sore as he stretched them, working out the kinks.

As fast as he was able, he crawled to the window of the van, looking for Carl. He managed to locate him just before he disappeared inside a small convenience store. Eli reached for the door handle, relieved when he discovered it was unlocked.

As quietly as possible, Eli slipped out of the van. With a quick glance over his shoulder, he took off running as fast as he could manage. At the moment, his fastest was more like a quick jog, but at least it was putting him in the right direction—as far away from Crazy Carl as possible. He could feel the drug burning away with every step he took so he continued to push himself harder, until he felt the last vestiges of the poison leave his system. Grateful to once again have full control of his body, Eli continued his pace for three or four more blocks before fatigue forced him to stop. Taking a minute to look around, he tried to determine where exactly Carl had taken him. He knew, instinctively, they had not made it as far as Mason—he would know his home town anywhere. After another ten minutes of ducking down alleys and peaking around corners, he found a flyer in a shop window informing passers-by of a community meeting at the local library for all residents of Hastings.

Relief nearly overwhelmed Eli. Hastings was not even halfway to Mason. Carl must have been forced to take a longer route to avoid being spotted by members of the Grand Rapids Pack. Understanding that it was only a matter of time before Carl discovered him missing, Eli knew he had to use his time wisely. He needed to find a phone. All of the shops in the area seemed to be closed for the night. While it was safe to assume the businesses on the main drag were still open, they also brought greater risk of recapture.

Eli eased his way through a multitude of side streets, searching for something out of the way that would still have access to a public phone. He toyed with the idea of just walking up to someone's home, claiming car trouble and asking to use their phone, but he quickly vetoed that idea, not wanting to run the risk of putting an innocent bystander in Carl's sights.

As he turned another corner, hope filled him. At the end of a dead-end street sat a small bar. The sign on the corner proclaimed it to be Rad's Rest Stop. Music from a jukebox poured out of the open front door and the delicious smell of fried food confirmed they were open for business. Eli just hoped there would be a phone he could use. As he approached the building, his wolf began to whine apprehensively. Eli wasn't sure what was causing the reaction and feared that Carl was near and he just hadn't sensed him yet. When he reached the front door, he was met with the strong, musky scent of wolf. Thankfully, it was not the scent of Carl but a stranger. This could either be very good for Eli or very bad. The possibility of an unknown ally would be a major point in his favor, but the possibility of an additional enemy to keep track of had Eli wanting to turn tail and run. Figuring he had more to gain than lose, Eli entered the run-down building and headed to the bar.

It was like any other small town bar he'd ever been to. A long, scarred bar took up most of the meager space with a few small tables littering the remaining floor. Smoke lingered in the air while peanut shells and sawdust covered the floor. Car racing and football played on TVs and country music pumped out of an ancient jukebox in the corner. It looked to be a quiet night in the place, with only a half dozen or so patrons scattered throughout the building.

As Eli approached the bar, the scent of wolf grew stronger. He casually scanned the bar patrons looking for its source, before finally locking in on the bartender, whose eyes momentarily flashed gold as he registered Eli's presence. Eli sidled up to the bar and made himself comfortable on a weathered stool a few feet down from the wolf. Forcing the man to come to him gave him a chance to evaluate him as only a Beta could.

The bartender was a little younger than Eli, maybe early twenties, just over six feet tall and had to weigh in at around a hundred and eighty-five pounds. The man had sandy blond hair that just reached his shoulders and a solidly muscled frame. His wary eyes were the color of early morning fog. The closer he came, the stronger the scent of wolf became, eliminating all doubt that this was the shifter Eli had scented outside. The younger man stood in front of him, placing a coaster on the bar.

"What can I get for ya?" The words were casual, but his posture gave away the tension that was flowing through him. Eli smiled, gently, not wanting to spook the poor man. If what he was sensing from the man was correct, he was a lone wolf, and would naturally be suspicious of any other wolf that entered his territory, especially a powerful Beta.

"I'll just take an ice water, if you don't mind." Eli tried to keep his tone calm. He needed this man's help and an agitated wolf would be no help to anyone.

"Coming right up." The man nodded at Eli before turning his back to the rail. When he returned with Eli's drink a minute later, some of the suspicion had disappeared from his eyes. He set the glass in front of Eli, watching him curiously.

Eli picked up his drink and took a long pull, savoring the taste of the cold beverage on his parched throat. Whatever Tracy had shot him up with had given him the worst case of cotton mouth he'd ever experienced. He sighed happily before setting the glass back down and meeting the younger man's curious gaze.

"My name's Eli. I've been through here a time or two and I've never seen you before. How long have you been in town?" He made sure to keep the question gentle, not accusatory. He didn't want the man to think he was going to be in trouble for his answers.

"I'm Ryker. Came to town about a month ago," the man answered carefully. "I spend a lot of time traveling. I liked the town and they were looking for a decent bartender, so I decided to extend my stay for a bit." He looked down at his hands for a moment, obviously nervous. When he met Eli's eyes again, he looked cautious.

"Are you from around here?" It seemed Ryker's curiosity had won out over caution. It got Eli wondering if Ryker had made the choice to be a lone wolf or if it was a situation he hadn't had any control over. It was something Eli would have to look into at another time, when his life wasn't on the line.

"I'm from Grand Rapids," he said, reassuringly. "My boyfriend owns a nightclub there you might have heard of—Sephora?" He watched Ryker's face as he realized exactly who Eli was.

Ryker cleared his throat, held out his hand and tilted his neck in submission to Eli. "Your boyfriend is known to a lot of people throughout Michigan. It's good to meet you. Anything you need, I'd be happy to help with."

Eli let out the breath he'd been holding. It seemed his risk had been well worth the reward. He now had another wolf as back-up if Carl should show up before he could reach Kellan. He was definitely going to have to talk to his mate about the possibility of adding a new pack member. He was pretty sure Ryker was looking for a place to call home.

"I'm glad to hear that. I've actually run into a bit of trouble and I could definitely use some help."

A small smile flickered on Ryker's lips. "At your service."

As quickly as he could, Eli gave Ryker a rundown of the situation. The younger wolf, immediately grasping the danger they were in, immediately grabbed the phone off the wall in the kitchen and handed it to Eli. Giving him a reassuring pat on the back in thanks, he quickly dialed Kellan's cell. The phone didn't even make it through its first full ring before it was answered by an enraged Alpha.

"Who is this and what the fuck have you done with my mate?" Kellan's roar echoed through the phone so loudly, nearby patrons shot Eli a questioning look. He merely shrugged indulgently and focused on his mate.

"Kellan, it's me. Stop freaking out! I'm fine for now, but I need you to focus, all right?"

"Eli? Thank fuck! Where are you, baby?" Kellan sounded like he was losing his mind. The low growl that followed hit Eli low in the gut, sending tingles down his spine and into his groin. Damn. The things Kellan could do to him, even over the phone, should be illegal.

"I'm at a bar called Rad's Rest Stop, in Hastings. Carl's here, too. I got away from him when he stopped at a gas station, but I'm sure he's realized I'm gone by now and is looking for me." He hesitated, the Beta side of him hating the words that were about to come out of his mouth while the realist within him knew they needed to be said. "I need some help here, Kel."

"Are you injured?"

"No. I'm okay. I didn't even get a chance to fight back, when they took me. For an abduction, it was kind of anticlimactic," Eli rambled.

"They?"

Blaming his exhaustion and annoyance for his loss of verbal filter, Eli winced as soon as the words had left his lips. While there was no love lost between Tracy and himself, he understood that Kellan had been close to the man for years. The knowledge that his ex-lover was capable of such selfish and malicious acts would be painful for a man who cared so deeply for others. This wasn't the way he had planned on breaking the news of Tracy's betrayal to his mate. Unfortunately, now, he had no other choice.

"Kellan. There's something I have to tell you about Tracy…"

Chapter Seventeen

Kellan's heart seized at Eli's mention of his ex-lover's name. While in theory, he knew Tracy was involved, to be faced with the confirmation that he had been an active, willing participant in his mate's abduction was like a knife in the back.

"What. Did. Tracy. Do?"

"Kellan..." Eli placated, his soft tone doing nothing to calm the raging beast inside Kellan.

"Don't make me ask you again, Eli." The seriousness in his tone must have impressed on Eli the gravity of the situation. His mate sighed and quickly rattled off the details of his abduction and subsequent escape.

Every detail Eli provided fueled Kellan's anger. His wolf was on edge, testing the limits of Kellan's control, and he had never been more tempted to let him win. The wolf saw things in black and white. It didn't care about emotion or rules. To the wolf, someone had caused harm to his mate. The punishment—death. Kellan could definitely get behind that plan.

Unfortunately, as Alpha, he had to set an example for the rest of the pack. One act of rage-fueled vengeance, and soon the whole pack would be thrust into chaos. He took deep, calming breaths, trying to ease the beast inside him. When he finally felt confident about the state of his control, he focused on his mate.

"E, are you okay?" His voice was so soft and concerned, he almost didn't recognize it. He'd never held even a fraction of the concern he felt for Eli for another lover. Over the last few weeks, Eli had become his world. He would do anything in his power to keep the man safe, whether he liked it or not. Kellan doubted he was ever going to let Eli leave their bedroom again once he got him safely back home.

"I'm fine. They didn't work me over or anything. Whatever drug Tracy gave me sort of paralyzed me. My run for freedom helped to burn off the last of its effects, but I still don't think I'll be running any marathons for at least a few more days. I'm just tired and sore… It's been a really long day. I'd really like to come home and get in bed with you. I can't think of anything more perfect than your skin against mine, right now."

Kellan could hear exhaustion in his mate's voice, but nothing else. The absence of pain in his voice, as well as the mental image of Eli, naked in his bed, reassured his wolf that his mate was not in immediate danger. Now, he needed to reassure his mate.

"Thank you for telling me about Tracy. He tried to cover up his involvement but he did a pretty terrible job. Maybe he thought I would be too distraught to notice. Regardless, I have teams out looking for him as we speak. His treachery will not go unpunished."

"Are you all right?" Eli's voice was soft and full of concern. Kellan appreciated it, though it wasn't necessary.

"Don't worry about me, E. You're the one we need to be worried about. I don't want Carl to find you before we can get there. We're actually not that far from you. About twenty minutes after we found you were missing, I got a call from a pack member who had been patrolling the edge of town. He reported seeing a van matching Carl's heading east. With the speed Dylan's driving, I'd say we will be in Hastings in about ten minutes, give or take."

Kellan spared a glance over at his Beta who was staring intently at the road ahead. When they'd returned to the Pack House, Dylan had broken down. He blamed himself for the loss of his Alpha's mate. He'd knelt at Kellan's feet and sworn a blood oath before all there that he would not rest until Kellan had his mate again. Jai, of course, had mocked him endlessly about being an "overly dramatic pussy," but Kellan had been deeply moved by the gesture.

"Kel, there's one more thing." Eli's tone instantly made Kellan suspicious.

"E..." Kellan frustration came through the line, loud and clear.

"I'm not alone here, Kellan," Eli answered quickly. "When I got to the bar, I scented another wolf so I took a chance and searched him out. His name is Ryker. He's a lone wolf." Eli paused, letting Kellan know that he was far from done. "I think you need to speak to him, Kel. I've got a feeling about him. He needs a pack and I think we need to offer him a position in ours. He's a good guy."

Kellan was quiet while Eli spoke. Ever since he'd met Eli, he'd known he was a 'fixer'. It was a trait all Beta wolves possessed, but Eli had it in droves. Betas strove to have a happy, healthy pack. If there was a problem, they solved it. Kellan understood Eli's desire to help the lone wolf. However, taking home a stray they knew nothing about could pose a very dangerous risk to the rest of the pack. As an Alpha, Kellan was the 'look before you leap' type.

"E, you don't know anything about this wolf. Talking to someone for ten minutes does not make him your new best friend. Besides, what would Jai say if he knew he was so easy to replace?" A low growl sounded from the back seat of the SUV where Jai now sulked. Kellan knew he was being an ass, giving Jai a hard time when he was just as worried about Eli as Kellan was, but he felt Jai needed to be taken down a notch or two for all the angst he was causing Kellan's Beta.

"Kellan," Eli growled into the phone. "Quit being such a douchebag and listen to me. Ryker is sticking his neck out for me and asking for nothing in return. I'm not even sure he would accept an offer to join the Pack. All I'm asking you to do is talk to the man, feel him out, and make the offer if you don't feel he's a serial-killer-in-the-making. I don't think that's too much to ask."

Kellan cringed at the anger in Eli's voice. The last thing he wanted to do was piss off his mate. Especially, since he had plans that involved his ass as soon as they took care of their current mess.

"I'm sorry, baby," Kellan offered, solemnly. "Of course I will talk with Ryker and see if he would be a good fit for our pack." He looked over his shoulder in the SUV to find Jai smirking at him. He flipped him off, before focusing his attention back to his mate. "E, I need you to grab your friend and stay out of sight until we get there. Don't make it any easier than it already is for Carl to find you. We should be there in a few minutes."

Dial tone filled Eli's ears before he had a chance to respond. *Well, wasn't that just fuckin' rude.*

Chapter Eighteen

After returning the phone to its cradle, Eli headed back to the bar and reclaimed his stool. Ryker took away his empty glass, replacing it with an ice cold beer. When Eli raised a brow, the lone wolf shrugged.

"I think the situation calls for something a bit stronger than water. Don't you?"

Unable to find any fault in his logic, Eli took a long pull from the bottle, letting the cool liquid settle his nerves. Setting the bottle back on the bar he met Ryker's gaze, smirking at the slight irritation he found there. *Good*, he thought to himself. *Nice to see he has enough balls to be annoyed that I kept him waiting.* The last thing the pack needed was a meek pushover.

"Kellan's a few minutes away," he stated, not wanting to push his new friend's temper any further. "He's got back-up with him so all we have to do is hang tight and keep a low profile for a few more minutes and this should all be over." He flashed the blond wolf what he hoped was a reassuring smile.

Ryker looked down at the bar, his whole body taut as a piano string.

"Did you tell him about me?" The words were quiet and filled with apprehension.

"Yes," Eli answered simply. He placed a hand on Ryker's shoulder, giving it a reassuring squeeze. "I explained the situation and how you offered to help me. He's looking forward to meeting you." Ryker tensed further at the words, causing Eli to chuckle sardonically. "Relax, man. Kellan isn't going to hurt you. You offered to help me, with no thought to your own safety. That makes you a friend of the Pack." Thinking about his mate, Eli chuckled again. "Although, I've got to warn you, he tends to be a bit growly. It's got to be an Alpha thing."

A hesitant smile crept onto Ryker's face causing Eli to smile in return. With the tension broken and help on the way, Eli grabbed his beer and motioned for the other man to follow him into the back hallway to wait for Kellan's arrival. Beers in hand, they spent the time enjoying the calm before the storm.

Almost ten minutes later, their calm disappeared when the sound of squealing tires and multiple slamming doors filled their ears. Eli met Ryker's anxious gaze and tried to reassure him with a smile.

"I'm sure it's just Kellan and his Betas. No need to worry, man. Everything is going to be fine." Eli tried to soothe the younger wolf, but found it was a lost cause when a familiar voice sounded out from the front of the bar.

"Eli, I know you're in here. Come out, now. Don't make the situation worse by making me come get you. And please, bring your friend as well."

Eli motioned for Ryker to follow as they made their way out into the bar. Re-entering the room, his eyes went wide as he took in the scene before him. Carl Yager and at least a half dozen large men stood just inside the entrance of the bar. The air around them nearly crackled with nervous energy and malice. Carl's face was stoic but his eyes flared when he caught sight of Eli. The other men's expressions were a mix of danger and hatred. Eli didn't recognize any of them, but he knew that if they were with Carl, they had been sent by his father.

The few human patrons in the bar, sensing something bad was about to happen, quickly fled the building. Eli didn't blame them. If he could have escaped from the knowledge he'd just received, he would probably have done so too. Giving Ryker a warning glance, Eli stepped forward to face the men guarding the entrance, forcing an expression of indifference on his face.

"Carl. I think it's time for you to go."

"Eli, you know that is not going to happen. I was worried when I got back to the van and you were gone. Why would you leave me, Eli?" The look on Carl's face displayed genuine confusion, making Eli fight the urge to shove his fist down Carl's throat. He had to remind himself that Carl was a crazy fuck and nothing Eli did was going to change that...even if it would make him feel better about the situation.

"You kidnapped and drugged me, Carl. Of course, I ran away from you. You are out of your goddamned mind! You and my father can go fuck yourselves if you think I am going to calmly sit by and let you take me back to Mason. If that's the plan, I'd rather you just kill me now." Crossing his arms over his chest, Eli scowled across the room at the men who had come to enslave him. He would not let them take him back to that hellhole alive.

"I am sorry for letting the little redhead drug you," Carl stated, simply. "You know I would never allow anyone to hurt you." He sighed, running a hand through his already tousled hair. For a moment, Eli could have sworn he saw a hint of sanity and regret in Carl's gaze, but it was gone in the blink of an eye. "You should have trusted me to take care of you, Eli. Now, because you ran off, I had to call your father and explain the situation. Alpha Steele is very angry with you, Eli. He has decided that, because of your behavior, punishment is needed. I asked him to reconsider, Eli, but he is very disappointed with you."

Eli sneered in contempt. The idea that his father thought he had any right to punish him was beyond belief. He took an anger-fueled step forward. "And what punishment has *Father Dearest* deemed acceptable for my disobedience, Carl?" Eli knew it had to be bad when Carl would not meet his eyes.

"A month in silver chains...effective immediately."

Carl's whispered words shocked Eli to the core. While silver would not kill a Shifter, they were all highly allergic to the metal. Exposure to it drained strength, caused severe rashes similar to third degree burns and brought on extreme hallucinations. To be exposed to the toxic metal for that extended a period of time would drive any Shifter crazy. There would be no recovering from the damage.

Eli fought back the shiver of fear the threat induced. He kept his tone flippant, not wanting to show his father's wolves how much the threat had shaken him. "Well, so much for father's brilliant breeding plan, huh? Guess I dodged the bullet on that one."

Carl looked at him, pityingly. "The breeding plan will go on as scheduled, Eli," he said quietly. Eli's confusion must have been obvious. "Your father has made arrangements with several families with daughters of breeding age. He has created a multifunctional holding-breeding facility within pack lands. The facility has specially designed...equipment...that will allow for mating to be accomplished while ensuring the safety of the breeding female." Carl's cool, clinical terms nearly distracted Eli from the magnitude of what he had just admitted.

Understanding, coupled with a rage Eli had never felt before, filled him, driving a howl filled with misery and menace from his throat. The sound was eerie, terrifying and saddening all at the same time. "You're telling me my father is imprisoning male shifters in silver, strapping them down and then sending females in to have sex with them?" His wolf's rage was a terrifying thing. Eli could feel it pounding against the inside of his mind, waiting for the right moment to be released. *Soon*, he soothed to his wolf. *Just a little more information and you will get the justice you seek.* The wolf, seemingly satisfied with the compromise, eased back, giving Eli the ability to think rationally again.

Carl nodded his head in answer. "You know as well as I do that, because of our mix of magic and genetics, artificial insemination rarely works. This really is the only way."

"You are raping them!" Eli roared, furiously.

"No, Eli," Carl denied. "They're men, for God's sake, and the females are volunteering in droves. It's not rape. Your father is merely ensuring the strength of our pack for the next generation. The children of these pairings will be strong, superior members of our pack. You must be able to see the necessity of this."

"No!" Eli snarled. "I don't see the necessity of it. What I see is my father and my birth pack condoning something monstrous. You are strapping males down and forcing them to breed with females, without giving them a choice. That is called rape, Carl. If it were the females being held down and forced to accept those same pairings against their will, we wouldn't be having this conversation."

Carl shook his head. "Eli," he placated, "they are male Shifters. You can't rape men. I'm sure they enjoy it. They are just being stubborn, as you have been."

Eli turned his back on Carl, not able to stomach looking at him for another second. The look he shared with Ryker confirmed their mutual horror and disgust at what they had just learnt. Eli was more certain than ever that his father needed to be stopped. Charles Steele was spreading a sickness through the packs, as was evident by the number of people willing to ally themselves with such a monster. The knowledge that there were other shifters out there who not only condoned, but also approved of something so heinous just further proved how far the sickness had spread.

Carl continued to drone on in the background, but Eli was done listening. He'd heard enough to know that Carl could not be allowed to leave this bar alive. His sins were too great to allow him his freedom. He knew he could take down Carl, but the odds were against him in this fight. Going after Carl would bring the goon squad down on his head and he had no idea how useful Ryker would be in a fight. He also didn't want to get the man killed after only having known him a half hour. His best hope was that Kellan and his crew would show up before Carl's meatheads had a chance to go after Ryker.

With Carl still jabbering on in the background, Eli turned toward the bar and focused on his shift. While most Shifters could only perform a full body shift to either human or wolf, Eli had mastered the art of the partial shift, or were-form. He was able to slow the shift to the point where he could shift certain parts of his body at will.

Keeping his back to Carl, he shifted first one hand, then the other, to claws. When that task was done, he poured energy into shifting his center mass to increase his size and strength. He felt the seams of his shirt pull tight as they fought against the strain of his new, larger form. His face was last on his agenda as he directed the shift until he had a fully formed muzzle filled with large, razor-sharp teeth.

Ryker watched the transformation silently, giving nothing away. If he was surprised by the partial shift, he gave no indication of it. It made Eli even more curious about the man's past, but he pushed the questions away, focusing instead on the threat at his back. He shot a meaningful look at Ryker, hoping he understood the gravity of what was about to happen. The man gave him a short nod and focused his eyes down at the bar. Eli followed his gaze and was nearly shocked stupid when he found that Ryker's hands were transformed into claws as well. *Well, fuck!* Eli was feeling more optimistic by the second. He flashed Ryker a wolfish grin and shored himself up for what was to come. He hoped that if he kept his back turned and luck was on their side, Carl wouldn't realize he was in partial shift until it was too late. Carl, in the meantime, had finally stopped talking and Eli heard the dull thud of approaching steps. Eli smiled to himself. *Showtime.*

Chapter Nineteen

Eli took one final pull from his beer before carefully setting it back on the bar. It was no last meal, but it was more than most men got at the end. Setting his wolf's senses on the enemy at his back, he took a calming breath, exhaling slowly. A heavy hand fell on his shoulder, squeezing firmly.

"I'm sorry, Eli, but it's time to go."

Remorse colored Carl's words. If Eli thought the man had even a shred of decency, he might have felt a little guilty about what he was about to do. Thankfully, he knew Carl was bat-shit crazy so he had no mixed feelings holding him back when he quickly turned, slashing out with his claws at Carl's vulnerable neck.

A look of pure shock froze on Carl's face as he lifted his hand to cover his throat. When he pulled it back to examine it, it was coated in thick, red liquid. A deep, spurting cut ran ear to ear on Carl's exposed neck. He looked up at Eli in bewilderment, hands shaking as he tried to put pressure on the deadly wound. Eli watched dispassionately as panic flickered in the man's eyes. A gurgling noise escaped Carl's throat as his head lolled limply to the side and his slack body hit the floor.

The only sound in the room was the low hum of voices coming from the TVs mounted on the wall. Eli's body tensed, waiting for the attack to begin. He didn't have to wait long. A howl filled the room, followed by the sound of ripping fabric and popping bone. The goon squad, reacting to the defeat of their leader, scattered, some beginning the shift into wolf, while others remained human, presumably to give the others time to finish their shift.

Not only did a normal shift take time, it also left a Shifter extremely vulnerable to attack, a fact Eli hoped to take full advantage of. As he ran across the room and into the fray, Ryker vaulted over the bar to join him. They ran into their first wave of resistance as the men who had retained their human form came at them, some brandishing knives, others using only their fists. Together they started working their way through the group. Wicked claws slashed deep through skin and muscle. Bones snapped and shuddered under their assault. The unshifted Weres were taken down relatively quickly, their vulnerable flesh no match for the sharp claws and strength of a wolf. Eli and Ryker also managed to take out a few of the wolves, left defenseless while still caught up in their shift.

Eli had just finished off his third kill with a mercifully quick snap of the neck when he was tackled from behind. His head smashed into the floor, momentarily dazing him. His attacker took advantage, raking sharp claws down his side and flank. Eli let out a howl of rage, as waves of agony shot through his body.

Quickly, he pulled himself to his feet. The wound on his side burned like hellfire and he felt wetness soaking through the tattered remains of his shirt. Shaking off the pain, he focused on the large gray wolf that was preparing for another strike. Enraged, Eli snapped his large maw at the beast, growling menacingly. The gash to his leg slowed him slightly but not so much that he had any trouble avoiding the wolf's next attacking charge. Eli neatly sidestepped the beast as it flew past him in a streak of gray fur. Turning sharply, it advanced, stalking Eli as a wolf in the wild would stalk prey. Eli would never be prey, a lesson he planned on teaching the enemy before him.

His muscles bunched as he prepared for his attack. Just as he was about to make his move, a high-pitched whine sounded through the room. Distracted, Eli looked over to find Ryker, bruised and bloody, pinned to the floor under the weight of a massive black wolf. The beast snarled, jaws dripping saliva, as it moved in for a death strike at Ryker's unprotected throat. Knowing he had only seconds to save the other man, Eli quickly changed direction, throwing the full force of his body at the attacking wolf.

The impact of the hit left Eli feeling like he had run into a brick wall. The tackle sent both him and the other wolf crashing across the room. Again, Eli tried to regain his footing, but his weary body felt like it was made of lead. His vision swam as black spots appeared before his eyes. A quick glance at Ryker told him the other man was in bad shape as well. While he had managed to right himself and complete the change to full wolf, he was struggling to drag his battered body to the meager shelter of the bar. Eli quickly stripped off the remains of his clothing and was able to complete his shift in mere seconds. It was a nice side effect that accompanied the ability of the partial shift and one that he was more than grateful for, given their current situation. He hoped the change might give his body an additional boost of energy. He could already feel his strength beginning to wane. Dread filled him as he saw the three remaining wolves converge, then split, locking in on their designated prey. One headed in the direction of the bar while the remaining two homed in on his location near the back of the building. They were in deep shit. His gut clenched as reality hit him. This was not a fight they could win.

Regret weighed heavily on his heart as Eli squared his shoulders to face off against the approaching enemy. There was still so much work to do if they were to stop the evil machinations of his father and his cohorts. He hated that his death would mean that the burden would fall on Noah and his brothers, to set things right. They would shoulder the blame and drive themselves into the ground to right the terrible wrongs their father was responsible for.

Looking to Ryker, he saw the rogue was once again on his feet, readying himself against his attacker. The guilt of bringing this situation down on the innocent shifter tore at Eli. Ryker was an honorable man. He had stood beside Eli, a virtual stranger, in a fight he could have just as easily walked away from. Eli could sense a great sorrow in the man and the Beta in him wanted to fix it. The fact that Eli would never get the chance saddened him. Ryker would have been happy with their pack, of that Eli was absolutely sure. Ryker needed a pack, and the Grand Rapids pack would have welcomed him into the fold. Kellan would have continued to give him shit about bringing home strays, but he would have accepted Ryker.

Kellan. Eli's soul cracked at the thought of leaving his mate this way. While he could never have predicted his mate would be a man, he couldn't imagine loving anyone else more. He didn't know when it had happened, but he had fallen in love with the Alpha. His biggest regret was not getting to spend more time with him.

As the two wolves began to close ranks on him, Eli pushed back his disheartening thoughts. They would only get him killed quicker. Resolving to do as much damage as possible before he was taken down, Eli focused on the enemy drawing near. While one wolf was considerably larger, the other moved quicker, his step more sure and confident—the mark of a rookie. That would be his main target. His only chance to survive this would be to even the numbers and pray for a miracle.

Eli charged at the larger wolf, momentarily surprising both his adversaries. Those precious seconds were all he needed. He feigned to the left, then quickly changed course when the other wolf went to block him, leaving his right side unprotected and vulnerable. Wounding the wolf would only get him a temporary reprieve. He had to go for the kill. Lunging forward with as much force as possible, he locked his jaws around the right side of the wolf's exposed neck. Eli bit hard, through fur, flesh and muscle, until his teeth hit solid bone. He shook his large head, tearing through skin and tendon until there was a large, gaping wound in his enemy's throat. Blood pumped thickly from the wound. A pitiful whine escaped its jaws before it fell to the floor and went silent.

While relief filled him, Eli knew he had no time to celebrate his victory. He could sense the other wolf poised to attack. Feeling the displacement of air, he tried to maneuver his body out of the way of the other wolf's charge, but fatigue and blood loss made his movements sluggish. Sharp claws pierced his shoulder, raking thick rivulets down his side. He howled, anger and pain blurring together to form a red haze before his eyes. He managed to evade the next attack and clamped down on the wolf's hind leg as he flew by. Snarling and spitting, the wolf rounded on him. Hind legs bunched under his body, the wolf leaped at Eli, landing heavily on his chest.

Fatigue made his limbs heavy, as Eli attempted to throw the beast off him. Feeling his strength diminishing, he knew this would be the end. Between the searing pain caused by his wounds and the copious amounts of blood leaving his body, he just didn't have the strength to continue to fight. He distantly heard the sounds of combat, confirming that Ryker was still holding his own. Eli's only remaining hope was that Ryker could hold on until Kellan arrived. He knew his mate would take care of the brave, selfless man.

His eyes drooped, as he fought to stay conscious. The wolf pinning him to the ground snarled at him, snapping its jaws only inches from his face. Eli knew he was trying to make him submit before granting him the escape of death, but Eli didn't plan on making it easy on him. The only wolf Eli would ever willingly submit to was his mate.

In the face of death, Eli felt no fear, just resignation and regret. With the last of his strength abandoning him, he felt himself losing the battle for consciousness. As his eyes drifted shut and he felt himself slipping away, Eli's last thoughts were focused on the hope that help would arrive in time...well...in time for Ryker, anyway...

Chapter Twenty

Dylan turned down the dead-end street and parked a few blocks down, leaving them with the element of surprise. Kellan was out of the vehicle before it even came to a complete stop. Running with stealth only a wolf could manage, he was within view of the bar in mere minutes. Any doubt he may have had about them being in the right place vanished when he spotted a group of Shifters surrounding the bar. They weren't watching the road for possible reinforcements, leaving Kellan to assume that their sole purpose was to keep anyone inside from escaping.

The reminder of what might be taking place inside stoked the fiery rage that had been building in him since he had ended his call with Eli, only minutes earlier. Kellan had hoped they would be able to make it to his mate before Carl was able to locate him but, unfortunately, it didn't look like luck was going to remain on their side. His focus completely on the men surrounding the building, Kellan felt, more than he heard, Dylan and Jai's approach.

"Six outside, unknown inside," he muttered to his Beta.

Dylan nodded. "Just got off the line with Malachi. Says he's about ten minutes out, with a team of five. He advised us to hold our location and wait for reinforcements." The look on his Beta's face confirmed that he already knew what Kellan would have to say about that advice.

"My place is with my mate, and my mate is in that building," Kellan replied pointedly. "Any questions?"

Dylan coughed. "No, sir."

"Good." Kellan turned his attention back to the men milling around the bar's parking lot. From what he'd observed, the men outside were not the most experienced bunch. Four out of the six didn't appear to be over the age of twenty-one. If he had to guess, Kellan would say the experienced fighters were inside, trying to bring his mate to heel, while they had left their inexperienced fighters outside as back-up.

"We can take them," he said simply.

Jai gave him a dubious glance. "Kel, we're outnumbered..."

"It doesn't matter," Kellan interrupted. "We can take them."

"In case you failed to notice," Jai snarked, "you and Dylan are warriors. I, on the other hand, am not. Gammas are all about diplomacy. We fight with words, not fists. Violence is not my thing."

Kellan pinned him with a steely glare. "It is today. That is my mate in there. Your best friend. Today, you are a warrior, Jaimeson Miller. You better damn well start acting like it!"

Kellan ignored Jai's wide-eyed look of shock. Maybe he was being a dick. Maybe he should be more understanding. Unfortunately for everyone else, his mate had been abducted and he wasn't feeling very understanding at the moment. All he was feeling, right at that very moment, was pissed. It was time to put up, or shut up, and shut up was no longer an option.

"Stay here. If it comes to a fight, surprise will be our greatest ally."

Rising from his crouch, Kellan approached the bar. With his head held high and a sure step, Kellan made sure he exuded both power and dominance. He was within ten feet of the group before they realized he was there, further proving their lack of experience.

"Stop where you are!" A tall, dark-haired man stepped forward. Kellan pegged him as the leader of the ragtag group.

"No." Kellan's voice rang out over the parking lot. He didn't bother to shout. His voice was filled with the power of an Alpha and the Shifters before him recognized the tone immediately. They began to list, side to side, instinct telling them to obey the demands of the Alpha, their orders telling them otherwise. An older, more experienced shifter would have the strength and training to ignore the power of an opposing Alpha. These men had no business being out in the field. They would be like lambs to the slaughter for an Alpha bent on their destruction. Luckily for them, all Kellan wanted was for them to get the hell out of his way, so he could get to his mate.

"I am Kellan Reeves, Alpha of the Grand Rapids Pack. I am here for my mate, Elijah Steele. He was abducted from my territory by a member of your pack and is currently being held against his will within the bar behind you. I do not wish to cause you any harm, but if you continue to stand in my way, you will leave me no choice. What is your decision?"

Nervous energy worked its way through the gathered men. It was clear that none of them were excited by the prospect of having to face an Alpha in combat, even if he did appear to be alone. Dylan and Jai were still nearly three blocks down the road. That distance, combined with the scent of smoke and stale beer wafting out from the bar, would successfully mask their presence from their inexperienced enemy until they were needed. As it was, many of the men were already looking around, as if planning their escape route. A few even took a step or two in the opposite direction, before their leader halted their exodus.

"You may be an Alpha, Kellan Reeves," their leader responded, malice dripping from every word, "but you are not our Alpha. We follow the orders of Charles Steele, the one true Alpha. He has demanded the return of his son, Elijah Matthew Steele, to faces charges for crimes committed against both the Mason Pack and against Alpha Steele himself. Now," he went on, condescendingly, "we will give you the opportunity to walk away, and in return, we promise that no action will be taken against your Pack...for now."

The smug look on the man's face suggested that he believed he had won some victory over Kellan. Kellan feigned a moment of thought before aiming a smirk in the other man's direction. "Tempting...but I think it would be quicker if we just kill you, and then get on with our day."

The man looked startled. "We?"

Kellan laughed. "Did you honestly believe I came here alone?" Tilting back his head, he released a howl so loud and full of menace it raised the hairs on the backs of his arms. The sound echoed off the nearby houses and buildings, seeming to grow in its intensity. That in itself might have been enough, but when two answering howls sounded in the distance, Kellan knew the opposition's numbers were going to be dropping soon. Just as he suspected, two of the men, no longer able to control their rampant nerves, made a break for the trees, not even bothering to look back. A few others looked like they wished they'd run, but after receiving an enraged glare from their leader, they remained where they were.

"You are a fool, Alpha Reeves," the leader, sneered. "To fight against Alpha Steele is to fight against the future."

Whatever Kellan had been prepared to say died on the tip of his tongue, as a pain-filled howl sounded from within the building. "Enough of this!" Kellan snarled. Without another word, Kellan shifted. While the shift, for most, was a slow, sometimes painful process, Kellan's shift was a wave of energy. It crashed over him, swelled then receded, dragging his human self away with the tide, leaving the wolf in its place. The change was so quick it was nearly over before it began.

With his shift complete and his human half gone, what stood in his place was a gigantic, brown wolf. While most shifters were slightly larger than normal wolves, Kellan's wolf was the size of an adult Siberian tiger. With wide, massive shoulders layered with muscle and a large, rounded head, equipped with fangs that would give a vampire an inferiority complex, Kellan was scary as hell.

While the other wolves finished their shifts, Kellan howled out a command for Dylan and Jai to join him. A moment later, two large wolves approached him from behind. A large, nearly black wolf led the way, while a smaller, golden wolf followed closely behind. When they reached his side, Kellan used the Pack bond to convey his wishes to Dylan and Jai. With enemies such as these, Kellan would prefer to try to keep them alive. He wanted them subdued or incapacitated if possible — death only as a last resort.

A quick look over his shoulder showed that most of the wolves had completed their shifts, and were waiting for direction from their leader. The man had shifted into a mangy-looking gray wolf, about the same size as Dylan's wolf. It snarled and snapped as its gaze locked on Kellan. He knew, in that instant, that the man would not allow himself to be taken alive. Death would be the only option. The thought made him sad for a brief moment before another sound of pain echoed from inside the building.

Kellan snarled in response, lurching forward, taking deadly aim at the other wolf's vulnerable throat. Only quick thinking on the other wolf's part kept the fight from being over, right then and there. At the last minute, he twisted his body to the side, causing Kellan to just clip the side of his neck and collarbone. The gray wolf yelped out in pain and Kellan growled in response.

Giving a full body shake, the gray wolf turned back to Kellan, head down and teeth bared. This time, it was the smaller wolf who made the first move, pain and fury making his movements sloppy. He dove at Kellan with claws extended, ready to strike. Fortunately for Kellan, the smaller wolf's aim was off, sending him careening to the right, missing Kellan completely. The wolf landed in a heap, right next to the open front door to the bar. A glance to his right revealed that Dylan and Jai had already managed to subdue the other wolves. Two appeared to be completely uninjured, while the third lay on its side, breathing heavily, blood running down its left hind leg.

A familiar howl from inside had Kellan jerking to attention, eyes back on the entrance to the bar. His combatant was back on his feet, though a bit unsteady, and looked like he was preparing to take another run at him. Kellan was done playing games with this whelp. His mate was in trouble. Calling out a sharp growl to Dylan and Jai, he charged the gray wolf before it had a chance to move. With its perfect placement, Kellan was able to drive it backward, right through the open bar door.

Following the other wolf through the portal, Kellan was met with a scene from his greatest nightmare. Eli was on the floor, unmoving, blood pooling around him, with a large wolf looming over him. He heard Dylan and Jai at his back, but all he could focus on was the image of his mate, still as death, bleeding out on the floor. The growl that emerged from his throat was a sound he had never made before, and hoped to never make again. The wolf looming over Eli, however, seemed unaffected, too focused on tearing apart what was left of his mate.

Hunched to strike out at the wolf, Kellan was unprepared for the streak of tawny fur that shot past him in a blur of fur and fangs. Before he even had a chance to register what had happened, the fight was over. A large brown wolf was standing over the carcass of the wolf who had been attacking Eli's prone form. The wolf's jaws were still locked around the deceased wolf's throat, his head shaking back and forth, apparently wanting to be completely sure the wolf was dead before relinquishing his grip.

With the remaining wolves either dead or incapacitated, Kellan shifted back, needing his human form to care for his gravely injured mate. As he stepped forward, a low growl alerted him to the fact that the tawny wolf was still there, currently standing guard over his mate's felled body. Quick thinking told Kellan this must be the rogue wolf Eli had been telling him about. Racking his brain, Kellan struggled to come up with the man's name.

"Ryker," Kellan called out, his voice clear and strong. He raised his hand, palm up in a sign of peace. "I am Kellan, Alpha of the Grand Rapids Pack. Eli is my mate. He told me about you when we spoke on the phone earlier. He told me that you've been on your own for a while and that you might like the chance to see how it is living with a real pack. Was he right? Would you like to come with us, back to Grand Rapids?" Kellan took a step closer, motioning to his fallen mate. "Do you mind if I come closer to check on Eli? He's hurt badly and needs to see a doctor. If you can shift back, you are more than welcome to come along. I think it would be a good idea for you to see the pack doctor as well."

When the wolf still looked hesitant, Kellan lost the last of his patience. Pulling himself up to his full height, he glared down at Ryker. "I understand you are trying to protect my mate, but the threat has been neutralized. You will let me see my mate and you will shift back, so we can take you to a doctor. Is that clear?" Power, once again, rang out in his words. The brown wolf shuddered, before taking a step back, giving Kellan room and allowing the shift to work through him.

Not hesitating for a second, Kellan darted forward, before dropping to his knees at his mate's side. Eli's body was a mass of cuts, bruises and contusions. The man was so covered in blood Kellan was afraid to touch him, not wanting to further aggravate his injuries. A warm hand came down on his shoulder, startling him. Expecting to see Dylan, Kellan looked up and was met with an unfamiliar set of soft gray eyes. Ryker. The man gave him a gentle smile before turning his attention back to Eli.

"We need to get going. I'm not sure how long he's going to make it with the amount of blood he's losing." Signaling for Ryker to follow, Kellan pulled his mate into his arms and rose to his feet. They made their way through the wreckage of the bar, sidestepping broken bar stools and the remains of downed wolves, before exiting out into the sunlight. Dylan jogged ahead to grab the SUV, while Kellan cradled Eli to his chest, praying to any God that might be listening, begging them to save his mate.

"You should be proud, Alpha Reeves." Ryker's voice was quiet and soothing. "I would have been dead if it wasn't for Eli. I've never had anyone willing to put themselves between me and danger, ready to fight to protect me before. Your mate is the bravest man I've ever known."

A small smile twitched at the corner of Kellan's mouth as he stroked the hair back from his mate's forehead. His eyes remained closed, his breathing still labored but steady. "Yes, he is," Kellan murmured, his vision blurring, as moisture filled his eyes. "I am so proud of him. I hope I get the chance to tell him."

Chapter Twenty-One

Eli woke to a world filled with pain. Every inch of his body burned and pulsed with an agony unlike any he had known before. It was all-encompassing and he wasn't sure if he should hate it, or be grateful for it. The ability to feel it meant he was still alive and that knowledge filled him with such a sense of relief that it nearly brought tears to his eyes. Eli's last thoughts had been consumed by his mate and all the things they hadn't yet had a chance to share. The knowledge that he had been given a second chance was more than he could have ever hoped for.

The effort it took for Eli to be able to open his eyes nearly dragged him back into unconsciousness. When his vision cleared, he discovered he was in a hospital bed. The room was quiet and dark, a fact Eli was extremely grateful for. He was able to make out muffled voices in the hallway but beyond that, the only other sound was the rhythmic beeping of a nearby machine. He tried to lift his head but quickly discovered that his body had been filled with lead while he'd been passed out. Never one to admit defeat, he rolled his head to the side to get a better view of the room. The sight that greeted him had his heart ready to burst out of his chest.

A chair had been placed at his bedside. By the size of it, Eli would have guessed it had been built for an elementary school classroom. Currently, however, it was filled, over capacity, with an extremely exhausted Alpha. The man appeared to be completely passed out, though how he'd accomplished the feat in that minuscule chair, Eli had no clue. The green eyes Eli loved so much were currently closed, with dark smudges beneath. His hair was disheveled, like he had spent the last few hours running his fingers through it. The big man was reclined as much as the chair would allow, with an arm and a leg resting on the bed. Eli didn't think he'd ever seen a more beautiful sight.

The exhaustion on Kellan's face was extreme. Eli knew he should let his mate sleep, but he had an uncontrollable need to touch him. Again, he tried to move and was met with the same results. A quiet groan slipped past his lips as sudden, throbbing pain encompassed his body. Kellan jerked awake with a start, immediately reaching out for Eli. The moment their hands met, the pain receded to a more bearable level.

"Eli." The reverence in the big man's tone made his name sound like a prayer.

"Hey, Kel." Eli smiled, gently. "Missed you."

"Thank fucking God," Kellan breathed, before wrapping his arms around Eli and crushing their lips together in a punishing kiss. Eli moaned into his mouth, overwhelmed by the scent and feel of his mate. Only his lack of strength kept him from climbing into Kellan's lap to ride the bulge he saw growing there.

When they finally broke for air, a whimper escaped Eli, causing his cheeks to flame red. Kellan's answering smile could have outshone the sun with its brilliance.

"Baby, you had me so worried." Kellan's eyes shone with unshed tears.

"What happened?" The last thing Eli remembered was passing out in the bar. Everything after that was a blank.

"By the time we made it to the bar, you were already on the ground. Both you and Ryker were in pretty rough shape. We loaded you up and rushed you both to the hospital, here in Grand Rapids, for treatment.

"How's Ryker?" The reminder of the young man who'd risked his life for a virtual stranger filled him with worry. His last memory of the lone wolf was of him bleeding on the floor with a massive wolf bearing down on him.

Kellan scowled. "Better than you. He's already been up and shifted. The shift took care of the worst of his injuries. I had Dax take him back to the Pack House to rest up. You are the one we've been worried about."

"How long have I been out?"

"About eight hours. They really worked you over. Even Doc was starting to get concerned."

Eli raised a hand to cup his face. "I'm sorry you were worried. I'll be fine. How's Noah doing?"

"He's awake," Kellan's said uncomfortably. "Doc was able to get him to shift, so he's healing…" After a pause, he sighed, deeply. "But there's a problem."

"What's going on?" Eli didn't like the expression on Kellan's face.

"Noah won't speak…to anyone. I had Doc examine him to see if it was something medical, a result of the time he spent with Carl, but Doc says, physically, he's fine." He scrubbed his hands down his face. "I'm hoping, when you're feeling up to it, you can get him to talk to you. We need to find out if Carl said anything else to him, during the time he held Noah captive. We need as much information about your father's operation as we can get, so we can start making plans of our own."

Agitated and worried about his brother, Eli tried to sit up. "How long until I can get out of here? I need to check on my brother and make sure he's okay. Then, I want to go home and get in your bed. I need to be able to feel your skin against mine."

The look Kellan gave him was pained. "The nurses were going to page Doc. He'll probably want to keep you for another day or two..."

"No. I'm going home, today, with my mate."

"But...you need time to heal..." Kellan tried to argue.

"No. I'm going home, even if I have to walk there myself. Now, quit arguing with me, and make it happen." Eli leaned back and closed his eyes, effectively ending the conversation.

A small smirk formed on Kellan's lips as he turned to go find a nurse. "As you wish, Alpha Mate."

"Damn straight," Eli murmured. Kellan chuckled as he made his way out of the room, ready to arrange his mate's exodus.

Chapter Twenty-Two

Friday night at Sephora was a madhouse. The club was packed to the rafters with weekend revelers, although, surprisingly, they all appeared to be pack members. Alcohol flowed and the base from the speakers pounded through the building. The cloying scent of arousal perfumed the air, sending the masses into a fever pitch. The private booths in the back were full and being put to good use, while the dance floor was well on its way to turning into an orgy.

Kellan and Eli slipped in through the back entrance and made their way to the bar. As they approached, Eli saw Dylan seated in his normal spot at the end of the bar. His face was a mask of longing as his eyes were riveted on the dance floor where Jai was doing some extremely explicit dancing with a beautiful, dark-haired wolf. Eli shook his head in disbelief. Despite Jai's apparent apathy, Eli knew him well enough to recognize that his friend had feelings for the raven-haired Beta. What Eli couldn't understand was why Jai was fighting it so hard.

A hush worked its way through the club as they closed in on the bar. Eli allowed Kellan to help ease him onto a stool, before the Alpha turned to face the waiting crowd. Everyone seemed to be holding their breath, waiting for something to happen.

Kellan's voice rang out, loud and clear, as he addressed their pack. "I want to take a moment to thank those of you who were able to volunteer your time in the effort to secure the return of Noah and Elijah Steele. Your bravery is a testament to the strength and character of our pack. I will never be able to adequately express my gratitude for what you have done." Kellan's voice, normally so sure and strong, broke slightly, causing Eli to reach out for his hand and give it a reassuring squeeze.

"I would like to be able to assure you all that the worst is behind us. That the actions of the past few days were the work of a lone, crazed wolf, bent on revenge. Unfortunately, that is not the case. Information we were able to glean from the madman has made us aware of a new and dangerous threat from the South."

Eli's heart clenched at the reminder of the last few days' events. Carl may be dead, but Tracy was still at large. He had apparently had some of his little minions playing lookout for him, after he'd left Jai's apartment. When his plan to feign ignorance of the abduction fell through, they had called to warn him, giving him just enough time to escape his apartment before the search parties arrived. Unfortunately for his friends, Tracy's plans didn't involve risking his neck to get them out of town with him. That being the case, they were quickly rounded up and were currently enjoying the 'luxurious' containment cells beneath the Pack House. It was Kellan's hope that, once questioned, they might reveal information that could lead them to Tracy's whereabouts. Eli turned his attention back to his mate who was wrapping things up, while he prayed for a quick resolution to this new conflict.

"In the coming days, we will be arranging a formal pack meeting to thoroughly inform all pack members of the situation, as well as our plan of action to deal with this new threat," Kellan announced. "More information will be available for you soon, but that is a matter for another night."

"In the meantime," Kellan smiled and placed a warm hand on Eli's shoulder, "for those who have not yet had the pleasure, I would like to take this moment to introduce one of the men you all worked so hard to save. Everyone, this is Elijah Steele, newest member of the Grand Rapids Pack and my one true mate." The silence in the room was deafening. While Eli had known Kellan's pack would be surprised by the news, he hadn't anticipated this level of shock. As they waited for a response to the announcement, Eli decided he would never complain about the Pack House being too noisy, ever again. Silence was overrated.

Thankfully, their wait didn't last long. A howl sounded, followed by another, and another, until the room erupted in the beautiful song of a wolf pack, a true sign of their acceptance and joy. Eli felt his heart swell as he looked around the room at his new pack before, finally, focusing on his mate. Kellan was smirking at him and Eli had never seen a more enticing sight. Waves of emotion surged over him, reminding him how close he had come to dying and losing his chance with the amazing man who had become his whole world.

His mate's thoughts must have echoed his own. Surging to his feet, Kellan charged Eli, tossing him over his shoulder, and pushed his way through the cheering crowd, as he headed in the direction of his office. Eli knew that he and Kellan should be out there, celebrating with their pack, but after his near death, Eli had been feeling a near constant urge to be reclaimed and his wolf would not be denied. Thankfully, Kellan made it up two flights of stairs in seconds.

Wrenching open his office door, Kellan threw Eli through the portal before slamming the door behind them, effectively shutting out the rest of the world. With slow, measured steps, Kellan stalked him across the room. Anyone else would have known to be afraid when Kellan's wolf had this much control. Eli, however, sat leisurely on his mate's desk, an amused smirk plastered on his face. The low growl that rumbled from Kellan's chest hit him low in the gut, his ass clenching in response. It was a show of dominance and a demand for submission.

Easing himself off Kellan's desk, Eli approached his mate slowly but without fear. There was no way he could ever fear Kellan, no matter how aggressive he was acting. As he drew in close, Eli could feel the heat rolling off the larger man. He wanted to burrow in close and soak up that heat. He wanted the big man to take control, to own him. Submission was something he had never thought he would be capable of, but when it came to this man, his Alpha, the act came as naturally as breathing.

Dragging a hand across Kellan's solidly muscled chest, Eli circled his mate, savoring the closeness after their time apart. He felt his wolf's need beating at his skull, but he pushed it back, wanting to prolong the experience as much as possible. Another growl sounded, forcing Eli to fight back a grimace as his cock filled, painfully tight. Damn, did he love that sound!

Completing his circuit and, once again, facing his mate, he stepped toward the large man, leaning forward to breathe in the scent he longed for. Feeling Kellan tense, Eli placed both palms flat on his chest before sliding down and around to cup his firm, muscled ass. He let loose a growl of his own, meant to entice and attract. Kellan's lip curled around a snarl, mere seconds before he launched himself at his mate.

They hit the ground, hard. Kellan's arms wrapped around him, drew him in close and took the brunt of the fall. Their lips met in a brutal kiss that had their teeth clanking together from the force. Their tongues mated, twining together only to be separated by the sharp nip of teeth on kiss-swollen lips. Kellan's weight pinned him to the floor, causing Eli to writhe and wriggle, trying to get the perfect amount of friction on his engorged cock.

Grabbing Eli's hips, Kellan forced him to still, growling into their kiss. A very unmanly whimper escaped Eli's mouth and he really hoped Kellan wouldn't tell anyone he'd made such a noise. His frustration grew as Kellan kept up the brutal assault on his mouth but refused to allow any touch from the waist down. Eli felt like he was going to spontaneously combust if his dick didn't get a little action soon. In his frustration, he nipped Kellan's lip hard, drawing blood. Eli quickly lapped at the red stain before sucking Kellan's abused lip into his mouth, desperate for more of his rich flavor. The bigger man snarled, flipping Eli over, face first onto the carpeted floor. A heavy weight was immediately pressed against his back and he felt Kellan's thick cock riding the cleft of his ass. Moaning throatily, he pushed back, meeting Kellan thrust for thrust.

"Please, please, please..." The plea spilled from Eli's lips, unrestrained.

Another snarl from Kellan and the weight from his back disappeared, causing Eli to shout out in protest. Large hands gripped the waist of his jeans, followed by the sound of fabric tearing, then cool air meeting his backside. His shirt received the same treatment and before he knew it, Kellan was pulling him up until he was braced on hands and knees. The sound of more tearing reached Eli then the weight was back, now gloriously bare, and a large hand was wrapped around his rock-hard cock. Sighing in relief, Eli thrust repeatedly into the tight fist, encasing him.

"You like that, baby?" Kellan's deep voice whispered in his ear. "You like my hand wrapped tight around your fat cock, jerking you hard and rough?"

"God, yes," Eli groaned, barely able to form words in the face of such intense pleasure.

Kellan smile against his neck. "I love the feel of your hard shaft pulsing and throbbing in my hand. It's like a hot piece of steel, burning me up. Can't get enough..." Kellan nipped Eli's ear, then quickly sucked the sting away.

Eli felt his sac pull up tight, signaling his impending release. Frantically, he tried to get Kellan to release him, wanting the bigger man inside him when he came. "I'm gonna come, Kellan. Don't...wanna...not until you're...inside...!"

Kellan's chuckle was dark against his ear. "Oh, you're gonna come, all right. You're going to come right now, in my hand, coating it with your hot, sweat cream. Then, when you've given up every drop, I'm going to rub it all over my cock, mount you then fuck you so hard you'll be feeling me for weeks."

Eli groaned at the picture Kellan's words created in his head. Kellan's grip tightened, as he began jerking him faster. Eli knew he was fighting a losing battle when Kellan added a twisting motion to his pulls. The pressure built in his balls, and his vision started to gray around the edges. With one final twist, Eli shouted out his release, spraying Kellan's hand and the floor with ropes of thick, white cream. Eli slumped forward, head resting on his folded arms and ass still in the air, as he tried to calm his racing heart. His whole body tingled from the force of his climax and Kellan hadn't even been inside him. He wasn't sure he would be able to survive another climax of that magnitude any time soon.

Chapter Twenty-Three

Releasing Eli's spent cock, Kellan used his handful of cum to slick up his cock. After licking what remained off his hand, he took Eli's hips in a firm grip, his gaze zoning in on that perfect pink pucker.

"I'm sorry, Eli. I can't be gentle..." Kellan murmured, positioning himself at Eli's entrance.

"Are you ever?" Eli laughed, eyes sparkling with arousal and joy. "You know gentle isn't what I need. Now, move!"

With a snarl on his lips, Kellan thrust forward, mounting his mate in one hard stroke. Eli let loose a hoarse shout, while Kellan grit his teeth, holding back one of his own. He tried to give Eli time to adjust to his invasion, but his wolf's call to mate was too strong to fight. Mere seconds later, he was pounding roughly into Eli's hole at a punishing pace. His mate didn't seem to mind, if his moans were any indication.

"So tight..." Kellan's voice was low and rough as he plunged repeatedly into his mate's welcoming body. "I love your ass, E. It's like a hot fist, squeezing me just right." Eli groaned again, pushing back against him as he thrust over and over again. "That's right, baby. Fuck yourself on my cock. Show me how much you want it."

The room filled with lusty moans and the sound of slapping skin. The fucking he gave Eli was brutal. He was more animal than man as he rutted into him at a frenzied pace. Leaning forward, he licked a line up Eli's neck then nipped a path back down. The wolfish whine that escaped his mate, only revved up his need to dominate the smaller man. He hammered into Eli with a force that would have normally made him cringe. A shiver up his spine and a tightening in his balls signaled his approaching release.

"I'm so close, Eli. Gonna come so hard... Gonna fill you so full of my spunk, you're gonna be dripping with me... You ready for me, E? You ready for what I've got for ya?"

"Oh, yeah. Kellan, please, I want it! Harder...fuck me harder!"

Kellan slammed into Eli, forcing his cock to new depths inside his mate. "Mine!" he growled. "My mate!" He made another pass over Eli's neck with his tongue before plunging his teeth deep into his throat. Eli's shout morphed into a howl as he sprayed again, coating the floor with his seed. His ass clamped down tight on Kellan's cock, setting off a chain reaction as Kellan's howl joined with his mate's while he poured his release into Eli's hot passage. Howls from the pack downstairs soon combined with their own, celebrating the new mating of the Alpha pair.

"Oh, fuck!" Kellan groaned, his head falling to rest on Eli's shoulder as he licked away the thin trail of blood that was leaking from his fresh wound. They lay there, chests heaving, still connected, until Eli started to lose the ability to breathe. He wiggled and whined until Kellan got the idea, rolled off him and lay at his side. A peaceful silence filled the room, both men just taking a moment to enjoy being together again.

Eli, being the first to regain some of his strength, rolled over onto his side. Kellan could feel the weight of his stare as his mate watched the heavy rise and fall of Kellan's chest. While his eyes were closed, the self-satisfied smirk on his lips let his mate know he was still conscious. Kellan heard Eli laugh, obviously amused by his Alpha Mate. Kellan was overcome with a satisfaction he'd never known before he'd found his mate.

"I love you, Kellan."

The unexpected words had the effect of a cattle prod, as Kellan jerked sharply into a sitting position. He watched Eli warily, afraid his mate was about to start speaking in tongues or levitating. When Eli broke down laughing, Kellan scowled darkly in return.

"What?" Eli questioned, innocently.

"Say that again," Kellan demanded, fiercely, a dangerous gleam in his eye.

Eli sighed, exasperated. "I love you, you idiot!"

Kellan watched him silently, for a moment, before a wide grin spread across his face. "Oh," he said, smirking, "that's what I thought you said." Lying back down, he folded his arms behind his head, the picture of relaxation.

Eli rolled his eyes then pulled himself to his feet. Searching through the clothes strewn around the room, he attempted to find something still wearable but found it to be a lost cause. Admitting defeat, he glared down at Kellan who gave him a look of pure innocence in return. Eli growled softly, more annoyed than angry.

"What?" Kellan asked, guiltlessly.

Eli scowled at him. "You know what. You destroyed all my clothes. Now what am I going to wear out of here?"

Kellan smiled. "You don't need to wear anything because you're not leaving this office until I've had my fill of you. I'm thinking a few weeks should be enough time to get more control over my need for you. After that, we can move this party back to Pack House and never leave our bed again."

Shaking his head, Eli walked to the door. Pulling it open, he shouted out to someone in the hall to bring them some clothes and a couple of beers. Closing the door, he turned back to Kellan, a serious expression on his face.

"Kel, while I'd like nothing better than to stay in your bed, or on your office floor, and let you fuck my brains out, we've got some major issues that need to be dealt with. Now that I'm home and on the mend, we need to start dealing with things."

Kellan observed Eli for a moment before groaning in defeat. Getting to his feet, he shot Eli a sorrowful expression. "Why do I have to have a responsible mate?" Shaking his head, woefully, he went to clean up in the bathroom that adjoined his office. When he re-entered the office minutes later, he saw a pile of fresh clothes folded on the corner of the couch. Well, no one could say that his pack members weren't efficient.

Eli was already clothed and looking very comfortable, seated behind Kellan's desk. Kellan dressed quickly, buttoning his pants as he approached his mate. Eli was shuffling through a stack of papers, sporting a no-nonsense attitude. Kellan smiled. Damn, his mate was sexy. He couldn't imagine what he had done to deserve such a man, but he planned to do everything he could to keep him. Lost in thoughts of how he could seduce Eli back out of his clothes, he didn't realize Eli had been speaking to him until he was hit in the face with a wad of crumpled up paper.

"What the hell, E?"

His mate scowled at him, annoyance clear in his gaze. "If you had been paying attention, I was trying to tell you that there is a report here giving a rundown of the Intel Dylan, Dax and Malachi have been able to collect about my father's operation in Mason and the outlying packs. I'm hoping Noah might be able to corroborate some of the info, but if I can't get him to talk to me, that's not going to happen."

Kellan watched as Eli frowned at the unwelcome reminder of his brother's condition. He was extremely concerned that his brother had still not recovered from his time spent with Carl Yager. Kellan had passed along what he had learnt from the doctor, but the news was a far cry from the 'sunshine and roses' they had been hoping for. While the external wounds had mostly healed, something was keeping Noah locked in his state of silence. It was worrying. To have Noah so unwilling or unable to communicate spoke of the gravity of the situation. Eli had been simultaneously racked with fear and guilt over his brother's condition.

Moving forward, Kellan cupped his mate's face in his large hands, successfully bringing him out of his dark thoughts. Looking at his mate, Kellan felt his expression soften and his mouth twitch with the stirrings of a smile. Leaning in, Kellan placed a chaste kiss on the corner of Eli's mouth. When he pulled back, he was filled with satisfaction when he saw that his mate's eyes reflected only lust and none of their previous worry. Standing, Kellan held out a hand to

Eli. "Come on, babe. Let's head over to the Pack House and see how Noah's doing, okay?"

Eli hesitated. "Kel, we have so much to do. We've got leads to follow, to track down possible holding center locations for my father's 'breeding' program. We've also got to find out how many packs in the area are involved and how far it's spread. We don't have any time to waste."

"Eli," Kellan stated, gently. "There is always time for family. The rest of this will hold until later. Dylan already has pack members assigned to investigate the situation and calls have been placed to Alphas that I trust, letting them know what to look for. Everyone is working on this, Eli. Now, let's go check on my brother-in-law." With those final words, Kellan strolled out of the office, leaving Eli to follow. He had no doubt that his mate would be right behind him, if only to get the jump on him when preparing to kick his ass.

Exiting the office, he headed to the stairs, turning when he heard his mate's clunky steps behind him. When he opened his arms, Eli smirked, allowing Kellan to pull him into a tight embrace. He inhaled his mate's warm, familiar scent, letting it wash over and soothe him.

"We'll get through this, babe," Kellan stated, fiercely. "We won't let your father get away with what he's done. We're going to stop him. I promise."

The words were spoken with such conviction, he knew Eli had no choice but to believe him. A ghost of a smile crossed his lips. "I know, Kel. We'll make him pay for what he's done to Noah and who knows how many others. He may be trying to build a strong pack, but we've got a strong family. There's no way we can lose."

About the Author

Born and raised in Western Michigan, JJ Black's love affair with books started young and has only grown with age. Always a fan of supernatural fiction and romance, JJ stumbled across the M/M genre and has never looked back.

JJ Black loves to hear from readers. You can find her contact information, website details and author profile page at http://www.totallybound.com.

Totally Bound Publishing

www.ingramcontent.com/pod-product-compliance
Lightning Source LLC
Chambersburg PA
CBHW020433180626
46812CB00003B/1216